Winged Horse of Heaven
Quest

R.S. McDonald

Illustrations by Trisha Romo

ISBN:0578144735
ISBN-978-0578-14473-3

DEDICATION

This book is dedicated to all those who worship in spirit and in truth.

CONTENTS

ACKNOWLEDGMENTS

Thank you to my very supportive friends and family who love Raneous and his adventures. Special thanks to Kim Clement and Lisa Bevere whose teachings helped bring depth to this story, and to my husband David McDonald who can praise the High King even in dark places..

1- THE MORTAL REALM

Raneous stepped out of the dense forest onto the damp cultivated field. He looked longingly behind him for the door he had just emerged from. It was gone. The door from the realm of the eternal Brightlands of heaven was closed. Raneous, a beautiful white winged horse, fought the panic that rose up in his throat. The door to his native lands may be gone, but it was okay. "I chose this mission and I'm here for the High King."

Now that he was once again in the mortal realm, his wings were gone. But Raneous knew that they were not gone forever. He had been here before. In fact, he had grown up right here on this small farm that now was just beginning its early planting. The spring rains had been kind and the field was full of tiny green sprouts. "What a difference from the last time I first saw this place!" Raneous grimly thought of the tortured, cracked earth he and Brian had worked so hard to plow. They had fought the Darkland demons and had won a great victory and now just look at the beautiful land! The land was now under blessing. He looked anxiously around, sniffing the fresh air searching for his best friend Brian. The High King had not told him how long he had been gone from the Shadowlands. Raneous was really hoping he would not find the boy an old man, but if he did he would just deal with it.

"After all, he's still Brian!" The whole time and space problem between the two realms was confusing to him. Raneous spotted a freshly painted barn that seemed to have replaced the old mule shed he used to live in. Ears pricked and nostrils flared as he heard some strange sounds from within its fresh pine walls. "I will check in there." Carefully, the graceful stallion picked his way across the field trying to avoid stepping on too many tender plants. He fought the urge to taste them as they looked so tender and green. "That would not do! Eating the year's planting before I even say hi! Anyway, I will have to get used to Shadowland food again!" Raneous pushed the images of Brightland's green, lush fields out of his mind. The High King needed him here.

"CRASH!" The sound of some large metal something hitting the floor startled Raneous causing him to stop short. The barn door burst open, "BAAAAAAAAAH!" A terrified looking sheep bleating at the top of her lungs came shooting through. She gave a squeak of surprise upon seeing the great horse standing in front of her and stopped so fast she sat right down on her haunches. With legs churning backwards, she tried to reverse her motion, and ended up right in the arms of the frustrated youth hot on her tail.

"Belle!...Gotcha!" The boy held tight to the panicked sheep. "Sheering doesn't hurt, silly girl! What's your ....RANEOUS!!" It was Brian, of course, and upon seeing the stallion standing so regal and alive in front of him, he released the squirming sheep and ran with outstretched arms, flinging them around the horse's neck! Belle happily took the opportunity to flee, free for the moment.

"You're back! Oh, you're really back!" Hugging Raneous fiercely, Brian practically danced in place.

Raneous let out a long, happy and relieved neigh. Brian was older but not OLD – and taller, yes, definitely taller. But the dark brown wavy hair, the warm dark eyes in the tanned face were young. "Brian! You're still here! I've missed you!" He nuzzled the boy's cheek. "How old are you now?"

"I just turned thirteen! But so much has happened I feel I have lived ten years since I saw you last! My mother remarried and my stepfather is great! He has really brought this farm back to life! He serves the High King and ...it's just amazing!" Brian's eyes grew wide in wonder, "The High King really did make things right!"

"The High King made things right because you made things right with Him!" Raneous gently nuzzled the boy's ear causing Brian to laugh at the tickly chin whiskers and warm breath.

They both stood there together just enjoying the moment and being together again in the fresh spring sunshine.

"Are you back for good? Did you get back to the Brightlands? Did you see the High King? Did you see your mother?" The questions began to pour out of Brian as the reality of his friend sank in.

"Yes, I think so to the first question, and yes, yes and yes to the rest! And before you ask me to tell you the whole story, I think I had better greet your parents as they just stepped out of the house!"

Brian turned with a joyful face, "Mother! Papa! Look! It's Raneous! And he's back from heaven! And he says he's probably staying!"

The two parents looked at each other and then questioningly at the magnificent stallion standing in their field.

"Why yes!" Becca, Brian's mother, exclaimed. "It certainly is your horse come back but I think he's bigger than ever!" Becca swept her loose, windblown hair out of her eyes as she studied the stallion.

Will, Brian's new papa, cleared his throat and looked at Raneous with his steady blue eyes. "You are welcome here always! The tale of your amazing victory over that demon Valtar has spread throughout this area. My brother was one of the lost souls you freed from that horrible prison, and it is because of his return and healing that I became a servant of the High King! Any servant of the High King is welcome here and however we can help you, let us know."

Raneous bowed his head to the two parents, "I am honored."

Will chuckled looking a bit startled as he had never heard a horse talk before. "I guess it's all true then about this big white horse...But I heard you have wings."

"They are there when I need them, but I would look pretty odd in this world prancing around in big feathery wings. I wouldn't fit in." Raneous gave a slight toss of his head. "It's kind of like a disguise, I guess."

Will cleared his throat again, stuck his hands in his pockets and paused to consider, "I have a brand new barn here if you would like to stay in there. I'd offer you a bed in our house, but it wouldn't fit you and I'd shake your hand… but you don't have any." It was quiet for a few seconds as they all stared at Will, and then the silliness of it sank in and they all laughed whole-heartedly.

Becca brightened, "Oh, I can make you some hot mash to go with some fresh hay, and lucky for you Brian just finished sweeping out the extra horse stall. Of course, we'll leave it unlatched, you being intelligent and all. But a dry roof and a warm barn is much better than a cold night in the forest."

They were still getting aquainted when all started at the sound of a shrill whistle coming from the opposite end of the field. A lone figure was stepping off the dirt road and waving his arms madly. The unexpected stranger began to run but with an obvious limp. Brian looked with concern at his parents whose brows were furrowed. Who could this be? And what did he want?

2- A STRANGER'S STORY

Will, Becca, Brian and Raneous all watched curiously as the stranger made his way somewhat painfully over the uneven ground until he got within speaking distance. Then Will stepped out protectively in front of the small group, "Ho there! That's far enough! We don't get too many strangers around here. What's your business that you seem in such a hurry?"

The man, they could now see, was twenty-something, average in height but with a powerful build. He was unshaven with several days worth of blonde stubble on his somewhat grimy face. He had a rumpled, unwashed appearance like he had slept in his clothes for several days (as in fact he had). His sandy blonde hair was dusty from traveling and sleeping on the ground. His right leg, just above the knee, was wrapped in a dirty bandage. This seemed to be the cause of his limp. He stopped short, with an air of uncertainty, but then seemed to gather his courage again.

"Pardon me for intruding on your land, sir! But please, you might think I'm crazy, but I have been searching for a certain winged horse and a young rider. When I saw this large white stallion here, I thought my search over." Here, his face fell. "But now I see that I am mistaken. I won't bother you any further." The stranger turned sadly to leave.

"Wait!" Raneous stepped forward and took several paces towards the weary traveler. "I am most certainly the one you seek! I am Raneous, servant of the High King." Then he added, "The wings appear when necessary."

Joy and surprise lit up the man's tired face as he realized the stallion was actually talking to him! The smile that broke out through the sweat and grime set everyone at ease. This man was no threat.

"Oh the King be praised!" the man said with hands upraised. "I'm Mick and I have been searching for you in hopes of getting your help!" Mick stopped and looked around at the group. Brian had come up to stand beside Raneous, and had his hand buried in the white mane. Becca had joined Will and they stood with arms linked listening intently to the newcomer. "Maybe we could sit somewhere where it's not so open?" Mick looked nervously towards the thick forest as if he expected to see someone or something lurking in the shadow. "I have had this nasty feeling I'm being followed."

At that, Becca came to life throwing up her hands, "I am so sorry! We have forgotten our manners, with you springing up so suddenly and we having just finished greeting Raneous ourselves. We are just not ourselves right now! But please, there is a table under a nice shade tree behind our house. You can rest that leg of yours and tell us your story and Raneous can be included - I don't think he will fit in the kitchen..."

Everyone laughed at this and it struck Raneous that he was truly a horse in a man's world.

"People don't quite know what to do with me!"

*

Mick was settled comfortably in at the big wooden table with his leg propped up on a three legged stool Will had provided. The two adults were sitting expectantly at the table waiting for him to say more. Becca had brought some fresh apple cider for the people and Brian had provided a bucket of water for Raneous. Mick kept looking with awe at Raneous who was standing calmly in the shade of the tree with his mouth dripping. "Still hard to believe you're not an ordinary horse. If I hadn't have heard you myself I would not have believed it."

"I have only now returned from the Brightlands and the fact that you were looking for me is a testimony to the High King's perfect timing! He truly is amazing! So tell us what made you so desperate to find me?" Raneous lowered his head to try the tender green grass at his feet.

Mick watched him in fascination for a moment before beginning. "I come from the beautiful city of Livia, the capital of the Eastern Region. Well, it was beautiful, but now there is something rotten and evil lurking there. Livia is at least a four day journey from here going east. The roads get better the closer you get." Mick sighed as he wondered where to begin. "I guess I will start at the beginning of the change.

Our King Jerald remarried after his first wife, Queen Helen, died rather suddenly of an unknown illness. What a tragic day that was! She was much loved by her king and her countrymen. While the king was still grieving the loss of his queen, a beautiful and wealthy woman named

Vanora, from the Northern Region, began to call upon the king offering him words of comfort and advice. Actually, beautiful is not quite the right word to describe her…mesmerizing or even hypnotic might work better - though she is very beautiful with her raven black hair and emerald green eyes. Anyway, she was very involved in her government and seemed to know anyone in power. Several months before Queen Helen's death, Vanora had become friends with her after meeting her at some social event and had sent some beautiful gifts; a silk shawl, a golden brooch..." Mick's eyes widened at the memory. "Come to think of it, that brooch was in the shape of a serpent...had beautiful rubies for eyes! I wonder..."

Mick shook himself, "No matter, it may not mean anything. The most notable gift was a bottle of perfume. It came in a mysteriously carved red box lined with black velvet. The bottle itself was made of hand blown glass that caught the light and threw it around the room in a rainbow of colors! When the topper was removed the fragrance of the perfume filled the room.

The queen was overjoyed with this gift and began to wear it every day. I don't work close to the palace so I didn't see the queen much but my brother, Sam, did and he started coming home with headaches after working close to the queen. He decided he must be allergic to her perfume though he absolutely loved the spicy sweetness of it. Not long after this friendship began, the queen's health started declining, and within a month's time, she was gone. The doctor's could do nothing and could find nothing really wrong. She just seemed to fade away getting weaker and weaker. King Jerald, in his sorrow and loneliness after his queen's death, became captivated by Vanora's beauty and brilliant ideas. She truly had a gift with words! Two years ago, he married her and made her Queen Vanora."

Mick looked around at the small group and sighed before he continued. "Not long after the wedding, the city began having problems with rats. They were odd rats too, jet black with yellow eyes. At first they were just a nuisance, but then their number increased and they were coming up out of the sewers and becoming bolder. Some of them were big enough they were actually killing the cats that were sent in to control them! The people of Livia began to grumble and complain against this hardship.

'Why doesn't the king DO something? ' and 'Doesn't he care about this city? We'll all die of disease at this rate! All he does is make ga-ga eyes at his new queen! He needs to take care of us!' and on and on.

The king was at his wits end. He had sent animal trainers and trappers into the city to set traps, put out poison, but nothing worked! The rats ignored the poison and avoided the traps! Finally, the king turned to his new queen for help hoping that with all her connections and brilliant ideas, she could come up with a solution. Well, she came up with a solution alright! I wasn't there in person but my brother, Sam, was because he worked as a spokesman for the king and he told me how it was. The very next morning, Queen Vanora walked proudly into the council room with a large python snake draped around her shoulders! Caressing its triangular head gently, she explained that the solution was easy.

It was easier to use nature's natural enemies to work for you and that all they had to do was release python snakes into the sewers and they would suffocate and kill the rats. She then assured King Jerald that since pythons don't poison their prey, they just squeeze them to death, they would not be dangerous to the people. And with so many rats around they wouldn't be going after the city's pets. Like I said before, the woman had a way of saying things that made everything sound so easy and brilliant. So of course, the king and all his counselors were astounded at her wisdom and enthusiastically agreed to this outstanding idea. And so Queen Vanora oversaw the project herself and could be seen thereafter in different parts of the city with that huge snake draped over her shoulders ordering crates of pythons to be opened into the sewer lines."

Brian and the others were listening intently to Mick's story and Brian felt a shiver go down his back. He didn't really care for rats but he was downright afraid of snakes. Not that they ever did him any harm. The rat snakes around the farm helped keep the rodent population in check, but it was something about their eyes that made him shiver even knowing they were harmless to him and doing a good job. He really preferred the barn owls and barn cats for rodent control.

"As you can imagine, at first it was successful." Mick continued, pouring himself another glass of apple cider. "But then we started having a snake problem. They were slithering up the sewer pipes into the houses and into the city's market places. The people began to grumble again against the king and his lack of experience." Mick sighed, "Livia used to be a city of music, culture and beauty. It seemed all of that began fading away as people started sitting around complaining about how bad things were going and that the city was going downhill quick. No one had anything good to say anymore. Several close counselors to the king began speaking out against him and that it was time for a new order of government. In fact, my own brother began to speak negatively about the king and how he had lost his edge.

The people of the city began to choose sides and argue amongst themselves. Then it started happening." Mick took a deep breath, "People started disappearing! I don't understand it and I don't know why, but Sam is now missing! Just gone! No one has seen anything or knows anything." Mick wiped a tear from his eye, "As you know, I am a believer of the High King, and I felt in my heart I needed to do something but I didn't know what. I asked the High King to give me a sign. The next day a young woman came in from a local farm to sell some apples at the city market and our eyes met across the square. She beckoned to me and as I approached her she looked me in the eyes and said, 'You're a High King's man aren't you?'

"My heart quickened and I nodded, wondering what kind of sign this might be."

'I am a prophetess, and the High King showed me in a dream I was to come to Livia to sell my apples in order to meet a young man there. I was to tell him the story of the great deliverance that happened in the Western region of the Borderlands in order that the young man might see the right path to take.'

"So right in the middle of the square she began to tell me about how a great white winged stallion had come from heaven. Also that he was ridden by a young boy. And how they had defeated a great demon that had built a great stronghold in that region! Immediately I decided I needed to find this horse and rider because in my heart I knew there was a mysterious evil gaining power over Livia and my brother and others were in danger.

That night I packed a knapsack of some food and water intent on taking the western road out of the city. As I passed through the empty market square I could see the yellow eyes of rats watching me in the dark. Just as I reached the city gates, I felt something cold and scaly wrap around my leg, causing me to fall onto the cobblestone street and cut my knee badly on a sharp rock. I turned to see a large python with a body as thick around as my arm! Its tail encircled my ankle! I grabbed a loose cobblestone and began trying to beat it off of me. Its eyes glinted red in the moonlight as it released me. Now I was certain that Livia was not dealing with normal rats and snakes. They were something evil and they were against me, and I must find the flying horse. Otherwise, Livia would be destroyed!" .

3- A LIVIAN'S INVITATION

Brian, sitting next to his mother, gave a low whistle, "Whew! What does it mean? Do you think the queen is behind all this?" He wrinkled his brow, "But why? Why would she want to destroy the city of Livia? After all, she is the queen, now."

Becca looked at Mick thoughtfully, "Maybe being Queen of Livia isn't enough. Maybe she has bigger plans..."

Mick rubbed his tired red eyes. "I don't know, but my brother, Sam, is gone and I am hoping that Raneous and whoever else would come to Livia to help me find him."

Brian's eyes brightened expectantly, looking at his parents. Will considered the situation. "I can't leave the farm with the growing season just started, but Brian has experience with this kind of thing. I can hire the neighbor's boy to help out around here 'til you get back."

Becca gulped, "But he's a child!"

Will smiled, "He's growing up quickly and he's ridden with Raneous before. He is, after all, the "young rider" everyone is referring to. I believe that this quest to find Sam is from the High King. We must trust Him in this. Besides, a boy and a horse will be much less noticeable than anyone else, really."

Becca sighed but had to agree. "But no one is going anywhere today! Mick, you are to stay with us. You need to get a bath! Becca wrinkled her nose. You're very ripe! And some good hot food in your belly will do you wonders before starting back again."

Mick beamed, "No need to twist my arm, ma'am. A real bed and a hot bath sound like heaven itself, but we need to leave tomorrow morning."

A cloud passed over the sinking sun causing it to feel suddenly darker and colder. Brian shivered wondering what tomorrow would bring.

4- THREE TRAVELERS

They were off! Becca had awakened Brian while it was still dark in order to get an early start. She had a backpack and saddle bags laid out on the table and had filled them both with supplies for the journey. Will had contributed a small roll that was a tent for two.

"Might keep some rain off you two in a pinch." Will offered.

Now with hot oatmeal and eggs warming the humans' bellies, and Raneous satisfied with hot oat mash and hay, they said their goodbyes and started down the dirt road headed east. Mick started out on Raneous. It was decided that Mick and Brian would take turns riding with Mick getting to rest his leg when needed. Raneous had insisted they ride him as it would look silly for two people to be walking all that way when they had a perfectly good horse to ride. So Raneous was saddled, but Mick just hung the reins over the saddle horn making sure they were loose and comfortable for the horse.

The eastern sky was turning a brilliant rose color and the first birds were beginning to chirp and sing. The spring morning was colder than it had been and Brian buttoned up the grey wool cloak his mother had insisted he bring. The fur lined hood he left hanging down the back. Very soon the road led them into the forest and began to wind its way further eastward. Presently, Brian picked up a nice, strong stick that seemed perfect for helping walk the uneven ground, for the road was full of ruts made from the spring rains.

"Raneous, I've been meaning to ask you something." The long white head turned to the boy. "How come everyone can hear you talking? Before you went away only I could hear you. Actually, that's not quite right. Everyone could hear you and understand you when you had wings, but when you didn't have your wings only I could hear you. What changed?"

With his tongue, Raneous played with the bit in his mouth thoughtfully and carefully stepped over a large rut in the road before answering "I'm not sure, my friend, but I have a good guess from what I know to be true. First of all, I made it back to the Brightlands and was completely restored to my true self. It is my connection with the High King that allows his power to flow through me. I am here by choice and have come back knowing who I am. As long as I have my spirit connected with his spirit, my true identity and his power can come through. For me that must mean that other people are able to hear my words. For you it may mean something else."

17

"I can have his power too? But I'm just a human. I'm not an angel or from the Brightlands."

"Remember your sword, Brian. Remember that you too transform when the power of the High King is called upon. As a servant of his you have the ability to fight darkness, but you also have other God-given gifts that his power enables you to use."

Mick was listening closely but at this he chimed in, "Ah! I believe I know what Raneous is saying!" At this, he pulled out a leather pouch from his knapsack and opened it to reveal five different flutes or woodwinds of different sizes. "As I said before, Livia is full of music. I am a musician and the way I best express myself and feel deep connection with the High King is when I play my pipes. I feel his pleasure when I play to Him! People say I have a special gift because they are moved by my music. But there are plenty of people who are much better musicians than I am, so I have come to believe that when I play with my heart to the High King, it enables His power to be felt by others." Mick selected a slender silver flute, raised it to his lips, closed his eyes and began to play. The sweet, clear notes danced out onto the morning air; the sun was rising higher and it seemed to Brian that the beauty of the sunrise was given a voice of hope and joy for the new day come - a gift to the world and to all that live and breathe! Raneous and Brian both listened in breathless awe as Mick's flute seemed to weave a web of joy and hope in the air around them causing their hearts to lift in praise to their Maker.

"Wow!" was all Brian could say as Mick let the last notes float away on the breeze. The man opened his eyes like he was coming back to reality, blinking a little at the sunshine.

"I don't always play like that. I can play folk music and songs of love and songs I learned as a kid, but when I play with my heart its like magic happens. I'm not so proud to think that it's my talent, because I couldn't play like that until I became a servant of the High King."

"But I'm not musical. The only thing I know how to do is farm work." Brian said with a frown.

Raneous nudged the boy's shoulder with his head, "Don't worry, you're still young. Your gifts may still be asleep or undeveloped. The great thing is the High King doesn't give everybody the same job. And who said farm work has no value?"

"THUD!" High and hidden in the trees several yards behind them, an evil, black reptilian creature with red eyes lost its grip and plunged headfirst to the ground.

"Blast and curse that flute!" The demon growled savagely as it dragged itself quickly behind a tree rubbing its head. "Sucks all the strength from me! I hate worshipers! Can't even get close to them now!" In its anger and rage it began to bite its own arms with its sharp crocodile teeth. "It's no use!! The Shield of Joy and Praise is over them!" It ripped out a chunk of its own arm flesh in savage frustration. "Ahhh!" Its red eyes gleamed with evil intent. "There is a way! Yesssss! I know another way!" The demon limped slowly deeper into the woods and northward of the unsuspecting travelers. "They will NEVER reach Livia!"

5- GYPSY'S ADVICE

It was early afternoon before the travelers stopped to rest and eat. Brian had taken the saddle off Raneous to let him air out while cropping the tender grass by the side of the road. Mick and Brian stretched their legs out on the ground under a big oak tree and dug into the ham, cheese and apples that Becca had packed. Having walked most of the morning, Brian was ravenous and was eyeing the package of ham when they all heard the jingle of a harness and the rumble of wheels on the road. There was a bend in the road so they couldn't see who it was yet.

Mick looked uneasily around and wondered if they should hide. But with Raneous' saddle on the ground, there would not be time before they were seen. "We need to be casual and not give out too much information about our business. And Raneous, don't say anything! I think we need to keep your gift of speech a secret for now."

Raneous nodded and wondered if he should try to look dumb but thought better of it,

"*I'm pretty sure acting is not one of my talents*".

Presently, a dark red horse with eye blinders shielding its side views came around the bend. The horse was covered with a brightly colored blanket with bells and gold tassels hanging off every possible point from its bridle and harness. It was pulling a brightly colored peddler's cart. Pots, pans, dippers, dried onions and strings of garlic swung from hooks clanking and clattering as the cart rolled toward the travelers. An old woman, wearing a purple hat with three green peacock feathers sticking out of the brim was keeping pace beside the cart.

"Whoa! Horse!" The woman said and the cart and horse stopped in front of the resting travelers. Her jeweled hands flashed in the afternoon sun as she fingered a gold medallion necklace around her neck. "Why, what a sad looking group you are! I'm sure I have something I could sell you to make you feel better!" the woman grinned showing two gold teeth. "Some tea? A silk pillow to lay your head on? A feathered hat for you or your horse to wear?"

Brian, who wasn't feeling sad at all answered politely, "No Ma'am, we are just taking a short rest."

The gypsy woman's face fell, "Oh? And where are you going? I might be of help to you still." She smiled again and fingered some long purple beads also hanging around her neck.

Mick cleared his throat and stood up casually, "I'm a musician, and we are on our way to Livia for the Spring Music Festival."

"Livia! Oh now, you are going the long way indeed! You will be so glad you met me! I caught you just in time as the turnoff is just around this bend in the road here. I travel to Livia all the time and there is a much shorter way. See, this road goes all the way around those small mountains you can see over the trees in the distance and that is long and boring. But you are in luck! Yes! I can save you a day's worth of walking. There is an ancient path that only the locals know about and it actually goes through those mountains - completely weather proof!"

Mick hesitated, "I appreciate your kindness but we don't have any lighting for cave travel and I'm familiar with the road we're on."

"Ah, but you don't need any lighting! The builders of this path placed openings in the roof to let light in. Very ingenious of them, I'm sure!" The gypsy flashed her gold smile again.

Raneous was listening carefully and observing both the woman and the horse. The horse was standing stock still, never turning to look at the strangers or at Raneous. The blinders on the gypsy horse kept Raneous from being able to see his eyes. *"Very odd for a horse to not be curious of another horse."* Raneous was not in the habit of being suspicious of people and the gypsy woman seemed helpful though odd. Getting to Livia faster seemed like a good thing. *"The High King could have sent her to help us along!"*

Mick looked at Brian and Raneous. Brian shrugged his shoulders. "A short cut would be great!"

"Of course! Of course! You will be so happy you met me!" the gypsy cackled happily. "Around this bend in the road you will see a large birch tree with white bark on your right. It is all grown up around there so you can't see the path. But if you push through the brush you will find some very ancient looking cobblestones that lead into the forest and up into the mountains. You will eventually come to an entrance of a tunnel. Follow it through to the other side and you will come out looking down at Livia in the valley. Now, I must be off! I have paying customers waiting for me down the road."

"Can we pay you for your help?" Mick offered.

"Oh no! Next time you see me, though, I'm sure you will think of something you need from me! Giddy up, Horse!" Horse, cart and gypsy started on past them. Unfortunately, the travelers never noticed one of the old woman's many rings. It was in the shape of a gold serpent with red rubies for eyes.

6- THE ANCIENT PATH

The birch tree was exactly where the old gypsy had said it was. Tall and beautiful, its graceful branches covered the road in green shade.

"The woman was right. There is no evidence of a path here." Brian said from the back of Raneous. By the way, who calls their horse, 'Horse'?

"I don't know. I know of cats named Kitty." Mick, not having any pets, did not think this particularly weird. "You two stay here." Mick walked to the base of the tree and inspected the thick brush. It was thick but not impassable. By lifting branches and pushing through for several feet he found that it opened up. Dusting the leaves and twigs out of his blonde hair, Mick looked around curiously. A dark red cobblestone caught his eye and then another and another. Yes, he could now see through the grass and undergrowth a rough path snaking through the woods towards the hills. "So far, everything checks out." Mick hesitated for a minute, looking around at the woods. Something, he couldn't quite figure it out, felt wrong. Everything seemed peaceful enough. He turned and pushed back through the hedge - which is now what he saw it was. It was wild now but may have been planted years ago to be a border or entrance to this path.

"Or to block it off from use." Mick considered the seemingly random thought but brushed it off as being too strange.

The other two were waiting for him by the tree. "It's just as she says, but it doesn't look like it's used hardly at all. Not too many locals know about it - except the deer possibly. I can't think of any good reason not to give it a try. It will be rougher going with all the loose cobblestones, but a day's journey saved sounds good to me too."

"Then it's a go!" Brian dismounted Raneous so they could push through the overgrown hedge easier.

The road, they discovered, was winding and was gradually leading them uphill. Brian remained dismounted as he figured they would not be meeting anyone on this path. Going steadily uphill all the time brought about more rests, but they continued to make good progress following the ancient path. As the sun began to sink, Raneous sniffed at the cold breeze that sprung up. "It may rain tonight. I wonder if we will reach the tunnel before night fall?"

They all realized then that they had no idea how far it was and that they had not thought to ask the gypsy. "Well, it can't be too far since it's supposed to save us a day's journey." Brian reasoned.

"Not necessarily", Mick responded. "It depends if you are cutting off a day on the first part or the last part of the journey. From her description, it sounded like that once you got through the tunnel you could see Livia in the valley below. So, we may be in the woods tonight. It's getting darker even now so we need to start looking for a place to camp."

The woods were very brushy, but presently, they came to a small clearing off to the left that was surrounded by trees. They were still going steadily uphill so it wasn't very flat, but it seemed sheltered. Brian got busy gathering some firewood while Mick pulled out a small shovel and began to dig a small pit for a campfire. Raneous felt rather useless at this point, but tried to help Brian look for firewood and began calling out possible selections. "Here's a good size stick over here, Brian! That one smells too damp to burn. Something, a hedgehog I believe, lives in that log." In the end, they made a good team and had quite a stack before too long.

"Now the tent!" Mick rubbed his hands in anticipation. "I wish I had had this on the trip out."

Canvas, poles, stakes, rope all got carefully laid out. However, neither Brian nor Mick had ever set up a tent. "I'm from the city, Brian, I thought you would know how to do this." Mick looked expectantly at the boy.

"Uhhh, well I haven't been camping yet." Brian looked uncertainly at the tent makings. "I'm sure it can't be too hard." Mick mused as he considered all the parts. "Let's give it a go."

The result was not perfect by any means. The little tent leaned to one side and to the back, but they could both get in and it was better than nothing. Mick had the idea of facing the opening away from the wind to make it warmer. This placed it facing uphill but that didn't seem to be a problem.

Becca had thoughtfully packed a tinder box and Brian was able to set the dry leaves they had gathered for kindling on fire. "I can build a fire, though." he said brightly as he warmed his hands and face over the dancing flames. After some dinner of ham, sliced bread and another apple - Raneous, of course, had grass- they began to relax. Brian gave the horse an apple for dessert. Raneous tried hard not to think about Brightland apples. Mick pulled out a wooden flute and began to play. Brian sat by the fire watching the yellow and blue flames while Raneous grazed just beyond the firelight. This time, the music that came from Mick's lips had a lower sound that had a longing, yearning yet peaceful melody. Brian began to relax as his mind floated away on the beauty of the notes. Peace and comfort seemed to envelop him as he crawled sleepily into the tent. He thought he heard an owl hoot off in the distance. Brian drifted off to sleep, "Camping's not so bad. I kind of like it!"

7- STORM CLOUDS

KABOOM!!!! Brian and Mick sat bolt upright. The lightning split a large tree limb not twenty feet away from the tent, and rain was pouring down. Thunder rolled and more lightning crackled and flashed overhead. During the night, the wind had changed direction and now was blowing down the mountain, and with it came a large storm full of rain and lightning. Already the tent was beginning to leak. Drip, drip, drip came from a few worn spots in the canvas.

"Poor Raneous!" Brian exclaimed and moved towards the door flap of the tent but Mick stopped him.

"He's a horse and will probably fair better than us this night."

Brian flashed Mick a dark look but stayed put." RANEOUS! ARE YOU THERE? ARE YOU OKAY?" Brian yelled at the top of his lungs.

He then heard a reassuring whinny through the rain's loud pounding on the tent canvas.

"See, he's smart. He took cover in some dense brush somewhere. Oh no...!" Mick groaned and scrambled to grab his bedding as water began to pour through the flap in the tent. "We are going to get soaked!"

The storm water was rushing down the hill. Mick's great idea of having the tent face the hill away from the wind now turned out to be a miserable mistake. With the door flaps facing uphill, all the rain water was now rushing straight into their tent!

They both stood bent over in the tent trying to hold as much stuff out of the water as possible. Maybe it would blow over quickly and they could relocate the tent. At that moment, like the storm knew their hopeful thoughts, the wind became stronger and fiercer. The tent, not very well secured anyway, started heaving and pitching in this new onslaught. Suddenly, a big angry gust blew the door flaps wide open. The tent swelled and billowed like a huge sail in high winds. With this sudden new force, the tent stakes lost their grip and the whole tent suddenly pitched over the back of the two camper's heads leaving them completely exposed to the full anger of the storm.

In less than a minute they were drenched to the skin. Brian's teeth chattered as the wind and the rain soaked through his clothes.

"Grab the tent!" Mick yelled. "We can use it for shelter!"

They both scrambled through the mud and rushing water to snag the canvas lying in a heap against a tree.

"Over here!" Raneous emerged out of some brush. "There's a big boulder over here that juts out of the hillside and blocks some of the downhill rain and wind." He picked up Brian's backpack with his teeth and waited to lead the way.

"I can get the tent! You go fetch the saddle bag. Leave the bedding - it's soaked!" Mick directed to Brian.

Soon all three were huddled in front of Raneous' big boulder. The trees were large enough to block some of the rain and the boulder served as a wall against the downhill flood.

Raneous considered the two miserable, shivering humans holding their sodden tent canvas and saddle bag. An idea lit upon his mind, "Mick, throw the canvas over my back. I will stand next to this rock so you two can sit against it. It will create a tent for you!"

"Not bad!" Brian looked up at Raneous' belly as the horse was standing over him. The large animal's body heat was actually warming up their make shift tent - Raneous provided the tent's support with his body.

"I sleep standing up anyway so it'll do."

Brian and Mick were not so lucky, but they managed to lean against each other and doze in between thunderclaps. At least their teeth were no longer chattering thanks to the warmth of the big horse.

*

When daybreak came, it was still raining. The dark brooding clouds seemed to hug the forested hills and continued to pour an endless supply of water onto the three travelers. They continued to sit in their little shelter hoping it would let up. Cold ham and an apple served as breakfast with some water from a canteen.

"If we could make it to the tunnel, we would be dry!" Brian said as he looked miserably out at the sheets of rain. He was not cold thanks to Raneous' body heat being locked under the tent canvas, but he was wet and itchy from sitting in wet clothes and shoes half the night.

"At any rate, we can't stay here all day, hiding like rabbits in our hole. We need to get on, rain or no rain!" Mick was determined.

Raneous shifted his weight and sighed, "I'm ready to move around myself and get breakfast!"

Mick suddenly stood up, pulled the tent canvas off Raneous, and declared, "Then let's get moving! We can dry out some other day, but in the meantime we need to get to Livia! Roll the wet bedding up in the tent canvas. Let's pack up and go."

As they busied themselves in the rain, a very large, very wet, black rat scuttled hastily across the edge of the small clearing back into the dense brush. Brian caught the movement out of the corner of his eyes, but when he looked, he saw nothing. Raneous stopped and lifted his head, nostrils flaring. He stood a moment taking in the smells on the rain soaked wind, but the rain washed all scents away. He sensed the evil presence but saw nothing.

The rat, safely behind an ancient oak tree leered up at the branches of the tree.

"Well, vermin! What news do you bring me?" came the raspy growl from the demon hiding in the oak's branches.

The squinty yellow eyes of the rat got even smaller as his lips curled in a snarled response, "All is made ready!"

The demon's eyes glowed a sinister red as he watched the campers. "They will find a pretty welcome waiting for them!"

8- MORE RAIN!

The path got steeper and narrower and began winding back and forth up the face of the mountain. Loose rocks, mud and water made the path slow going and dangerous. The three, Mick leading, Brian second and Raneous bringing up the rear, slogged ever upward while thunder rolled and lightning crackled overhead.

"You know, it's not a good idea to be on a high point in a lightning storm." Brian noted as he looked uneasily up at the angry sky. "Luckily the trees are still taller than us. I sure hope this short cut is worth the trouble it's been."

33

"Oh joy! Another wave of hard rain!" moaned Mick as the sheets of rain burst into big hard drops pelting the travelers and stinging their eyes. "And the wind is back!" Nobody could get any wetter at this point, but the stinging and whipping of the rain and wind was maddening.

With heads down they slowly pushed their way forward trying to step carefully in the rocks, mud and rushing water.

"STOP!!!" Raneous screamed from the back.

Brian looked up just in time to yank Mick backwards as a large boulder, the size of a small cart, came bouncing and crashing down the mountainside. One more step forward and it would have crushed Mick!

But before they could congratulate themselves for avoiding certain death, Brian gave a yelp as the path gave way under his feet and he began to slide downhill. Quick as a whip, Mick grabbed for him and managed to grasp the hood of his cloak with one hand. The angle being awkward, he began to topple over but Raneous snatched hold of his belt with his teeth and held fast.

"Can you get your footing?" Mick asked through gritted teeth as he strained to keep his grip on Brian's hood.

Brian was dangling in somewhat of a choke-hold by his cloak, as he floundered around trying to find something solid to step on. "Everything is mush!" he sputtered back.

Mick twisted around and was able to get a second hand on Brian's hood. "Pull, Raneous!"

Raneous pulled and slowly they were able to get Brian back onto the narrow path.

They all stood a little shaken trying to catch their breath.

"Thanks guys! I was a goner for sure!" Mick rubbed his whiskered chin uneasily.

"Yeah, thanks!" Brian gulped. A long slide down the mountain may have ended in some broken bones for him as well.

Mick eyed the narrow trail as it snaked upward. "I'm beginning to think we've been led wrong by our gypsy woman. It's been tickling the back of my mind for awhile but I couldn't figure out what wasn't adding up."

Raneous and Brian stared at him. "Speak! What do you mean?" Raneous asked.

"There is no way that a horse pulling a gypsy cart could make it up this trail - even in perfect weather! It's too narrow! That woman travels around selling her goods so she has to have her wagon with her all the time. Those people live in those wagons. Not only that, but I doubt she would be able to travel this path, as rugged and steep as it is, at her age. We've been tricked! And I should've seen it!" Mick punched his fist into his hand in frustration. "I kept having this funny feeling that something wasn't right, but I ignored it! Who knows where this leads?"

Another crack of lightning crashed overhead feeling dangerously too close.

"We have to keep moving!" Raneous urged. "We aren't safe here!"

Just then, a low rumble caught Raneous' ears and he looked up to see trees, rocks, and a river of mud sliding towards him in a gooey, deadly mass. One large pine tree hit a big rock and splintered in half with a deafening C-R-A-C-K! But the mass kept moving downward carrying the splintered tree with it.

"Mud slide! Run!" Raneous again sounded the alarm and began to push Brian forward with the butt of his head. "The whole side of the mountain is coming down!"

They ran or at least they tried. Mick, in the lead, squinted up ahead through the pelting rain. Something dark was in the path ahead. What was it? Black and round it stood. Mick suddenly understood. He looked up at the moving hillside. They would barely have time. "Faster guys!" Mick puffed. "The tunnel! I see the tunnel up ahead!"

With a new surge of strength brought on by both fear and hope, the three ran and stumbled as fast as they could with burning lungs and the sound of the mudslide rumbling in their ears. Rocks and debris were falling and bouncing around them and with one last push from Raneous, they stumbled into the entrance of the tunnel.

Raneous heard Mick give a surprised shout from the gloom ahead.

The horse looked up from his hard push just in time to see the shocked and terrified face of Brian before he too screamed and disappeared from sight.

9- TRAPPED!

Raneous stopped at the entrance, breathing hard and trying to adjust his eyes to the gloom of the tunnel. His friends were nowhere in sight! Panic rose inside and his legs began to quiver.

"Brian! Mick! Where are you?" he called desperately. His words echoed off the walls strangely. To his great relief he got an answer.

"Here! We're down here!" Mick's voice seemed faint and far away.

"We're okay!" Brian sounded frightened and strangely distant.

Raneous could now see that he was standing at the edge of a huge, dark pit! It's mouth stretched from wall to wall so there was no way to get around it. The sides were sloped so thankfully Mick and Brian had slid down to the bottom as if on a big slide. However, the walls were perfectly smooth and steep and impossible to climb. It was so black that he could not see the bottom when he peered carefully over the edge.

"Stay back from the edge!" Mick called from the bottom.

Down in the pit Brian had slid into Mick but luckily neither was hurt. As Mick looked up, he could see that the pit was "V" shaped. Something crunched under their feet and upon inspection in the dim light, they discovered scattered bones of other unfortunate victims. Whether they were animal or human bones neither Mick nor Brian cared to find out.

"The ropes from the tent!" Brian turned to Mick. "Do you think Raneous could get to them?" Without waiting for an answer, Brian yelled up to Raneous, "Can you get to the ropes? Maybe we could climb up them."

Raneous turned and eyed the tent bundle that he was carrying on his back. The whole thing had been tied up with one of the tent's ropes. Could he reach it? Raneous strained his neck back but could not reach the bundle. He snorted in disgust.

"This is ridiculous! Never felt so helpless in my life!" Determined, he reared up on his hind legs and gave a hop and then another hop. Sure enough, the tent bundle rolled off and onto the dirt.

"Now, this is better!" He nosed the bundle until he found the end of the rope. "Thank the High King it's not knotted!" Raneous gently lipped the tip of the rope and carefully pulled. Success! The rope unwound from the bundle!

"I've got the rope!"

"Can you hold it while throwing it over the edge?" Mick called back hopefully.

Raneous carefully clamped the end securely in his teeth and flipped the rest of it over the edge with a flick of his head.

The two below watched it, but their hearts sank. It was too short - way too short in fact.

Mick stood looking up and thinking hard. "What about the rest of the tent rope? Can we get them tied together?"

"Raneous can't tie knots I'm afraid." Brian answered glumly.

Mick eyed the sides of the pit trying to guess their height. "It's no use anyway. The tent's ropes are just too short - even if we strung them together. These walls have got to be over fifty feet."

Brian's eyes got big. "What are we going to do? I mean, there's got to be a way!" He stepped towards the slippery slope and as he did a loud crunch sounded at his feet. He looked down to see the remains of a human ribcage.

"NO! This can't be happening! It can't end this way! We've got to think!" Brian furrowed his brow in concentration. "We can send Raneous for help! Wait!" Brian's face lit up with a wide grin. "That's it! We have completely forgotten that Raneous is a flying horse!"

"The High King be praised! I forgot too!" Mick clapped his hands together in joy and relief.

"Raneous! You need to get your wings!" Brian yelled up excitedly.

Up top Raneous had been waiting dejectedly feeling like a worthless animal in a man's world. In reality, he would not have been able to help his friends even if he were human.

When he heard Brian's directions, he let out a whinny of happiness. How could he have been so stupid? Of course, he was a flying horse! He had gotten so used to plodding around on his four legs comfortably grounded that he had forgotten who he was!

"My High King, I need my wings, please!"

Nothing happened.

"I am Raneous true servant of the High King!" Raneous said in a commanding voice.

His voice echoed back at him seeming to mock him. No wings. Then it hit Raneous." *I don't know how to get my wings at will! The Power has always come upon me when I was fighting a demon! Maybe that's the only way I can fly?*"

Raneous looked around hopefully. Maybe a demon would show up now that his friends were trapped. Nothing stirred. Raneous also realized it was getting darker. What little light there was outside was fading. His heart sank. Night would be upon them and his friends were stuck. He would have to go for help. Concerned, he looked out of the entrance. The rain was still coming down. The trail was washed out about a hundred feet back where the mud slide had devoured it. It would be risky at best.

"I will have to go for help. I...I don't know how to get my wings to come!"

CRASH! A huge boulder fell into the mouth of the tunnel. An avalanche of rocks and mud came pouring into the tunnel entrance quickly filling it up before the horse could react, but before the last bit of light disappeared Raneous heard an evil scream pierce the air, "You're not going anywhere -EVER!!!!"

10- SONGS IN DARKNESS

Raneous opened his eyes and blinked. He had exhausted himself pounding against the caved in tunnel entrance for hours last night. It had been no use. Again and again he hit it, first with his front hooves and then with his back ones, but the wall of rock was too thick for even his powerful legs to break through. As the blackness of the night had settled over the travelers, a sense of hopelessness seemed to cover them like a suffocating blanket.

Raneous, as he blinked, realized that it was not pitch black as it had been. There was light coming in from somewhere. "I guess the gypsy was right about there being light in the tunnel."

There was no sound coming from the pit where his friends were trapped. Despair and hopelessness pressed in upon the big horse to the point that he felt like dying.

"I'm a complete failure! I don't know what I'm doing. Why did the High King think I was capable of this task? High King, where are you?"

"Focus on Me."

Raneous lifted his head and his heart quickened. He looked around at the hopeless situation, but then shut his eyes. He thought of the High King laughing with him as they played tag with the children. He thought of his wonderful loving eyes full of wisdom and the smile that melted Raneous' heart each time he saw it - especially when it was directed at him!

Hope began to fill his heart and soul driving back the despair. *"I am not forgotten!"* his heart sang.

"Praise Me and I will lift you up out of the pit of despair. See my victory!"

He knew what to do! Raneous gave a big body shake with a snort. Feeling his head clear, Raneous reared up pawing at the air and let out a high whinny of victory. "The High King rules! The High King is bigger than anything that darkness can throw at me!"

Brian and Mick were roused out of their exhausted and hopeless slumber by the sound of a Brightlander's praise. They both shook themselves as if coming out of a trance. Scrambling to their feet, they looked up in wonder as they listened.

"The High King is the Maker of all and nothing can stand against him and win!" Raneous shouted to the tunnel walls. "Brian! Mick! Praise your King and he will bring us victory!"

Not knowing what else to do, Brian shouted, "The King reigns! The King reigns!"

Mick joined in along with Brian. "The King reigns! The King reigns! The King reigns!"

Suddenly, Raneous felt the POWER of the High King flow through him and the light of the heavens radiated out of him in shining glory. His magnificent wings flapped powerfully from his shoulders. Raneous was his true self once again!

"For the High King!" he shouted and launched himself into the dark pit. Carefully, he descended down and landed easily beside his two joyful friends.

"Climb on, both of you!"

Brian first, and then Mick, scrambled up and held on tight. Slowly, and with care, Raneous ascended up and out of the pit. They were free!

Whooping and hollering, they landed safely on the far side of the pit.

"Wait!" Brian, exclaimed. "Our tent! It's still on the other side of the pit!"

"No problem!" Raneous laughed and with a flying leap landed effortlessly beside the abandoned tent roll. Brian hastily scrambled down and quickly had everything tied and loaded onto Raneous' back within a minute or two. They paused and considered the caved in tunnel entrance.

"It seems our choice has been made for us." Mick said thoughtfully. "We must find our way through this mountain. Who knows, maybe the gypsy was telling the truth about Livia being just on the other side."

"Mount up then, Brian." Raneous nudged his young friend's elbow. When both were settled, the stallion took another flying leap over the pit back to the other side. "The ceiling is too low to really fly in here without possibly bashing your heads or my wings on rock, so I think it's smarter to continue walking the old fashioned way."

Reluctantly, Brian and Mick agreed. What fun it would be to just finish the journey on the back of a flying horse! Mick stepped back and looked at Raneous in awe. He took in the magnificent and powerful wings, shining mane, and the glowing light that surrounded him. "You really aren't from here, are you? I feel like I've touched a slice of heaven! You have made the reality of heaven become...well, more real - not just something we sing about, but a real and beautiful place."

Raneous thought for a moment, "As a Brightlander, I never doubted that the Shadowlands existed but I think that's because I knew others who had been there and I knew I would be going there too. For you it has been different, I think. Until now, you have known no one who has even visited the Brightlands." Raneous paused searching for the right expression. He brightened, "It's just like the bottom of a deep ocean, or a far away country that you have never seen. You've never been there but you know it exists. Heaven is like that. It exists just as much as the strange and beautiful creatures that live at the bottom of the ocean or that live in a far away land that you have not seen or may never see."

Brian and Mick both nodded thoughtfully. Mick smiled with a new light of understanding glowing on his face.

"Well then, let's keep moving! Our King is with us! Onward through this tunnel we go!"

The travelers started off again with light hearts and renewed strength. Presently, they noticed the glow of Raneous diminish and as Brian glanced over to the tall stallion, he saw the feathered wings fade from view.

Raneous glanced at the boy and slowly winked. " Back in my disguise, I guess. The King knows best. Not to be a bother, but are there by any chance any apples left?"

Brian laughed. "You're so...normal! Yes, I think there are." He rummaged through the saddlebag that was draped across the horse's back and pulled out the last two apples. "Geez! I'm hungry too!" He continued searching the bag as they walked side by side. "Mick, you and I can share the last of the ham and cheese here."

"Let's just eat while we walk. We wasted a whole day with our "shortcut"!" Mick grimaced in frustration. "All night sitting at the bottom of that pit I ran through all of our decisions - my decisions to take this road. There were clues I would have seen if I would have not been in such a hurry to save time. Like, the hedge blocking this ancient road. Maybe it was blocked for a reason? Why didn't I think about it? And worse, I actually did have the thought but I brushed it aside ignoring the fact that this path - even from the beginning- had a bad feel to it.

And of course the width of the path was all wrong. Why, even in the beginning it was near impossible for a gypsy cart to get through without breaking a wheel. 'I use this road all the time!' the gypsy said. My eye she does! It was fishy from the start but I was too stubborn to see it."

"None of us saw it, Mick!" Raneous answered. "We are all responsible in some way for not being more attentive - or just plain clueless," he added thinking about his own assumptions.

Brian brightened up, "But the High King helped us even if it was our own stupidity! That's the best part!"

"Yes...yes you're right there, I'm sure." Mick admitted. "But let's try to learn from this. I for one am going to be a little more cautious from here on out!"

They all heartily agreed to that, as they continued to make their way through the tunnel munching on the last of their food rations. This was somewhat of a worry to them but they were all hoping the gypsy had at least not lied about Livia being on the other side. The tunnel proved to be smooth going and was indeed dimly lit by shafts bored through to the outside. They came across one shaft that was low enough to actually inspect with the thought of Brian crawling up through it to see where they were. It was hopelessly too small and Brian was privately glad as he was not hungry or thirsty enough yet to really want to crawl into an unknown hole to possibly meet up with who knows what creepy things.

And creepy things were in fact living in this tunnel with convenient openings to the outside. Bats hung from the ceiling, spiders spun webs in corners, bugs with lots of legs crawled along the walls, and mice scurried into dark crevices, but Raneous did not sense evil in any of them. They were normal creatures of the Shadowlands and therefore did not concern him. Brian, however, asked Mick to play a tune to help keep his mind off the creepy-crawlers. He was doing pretty well until he felt his right foot sink into something squishy.

"Ugg! What is it??" Brian pulled his boot out of it grimacing.

Mick inspected the pile, "Guano, or bat dung." He looked up at the not so high ceiling. "Yup, nice gathering of bats through here so watch your step."

Brian looked up at the hundreds of small bats hanging by their toes. Some were sleeping, some were wiggling their small, slightly piggish noses at him, some grooming themselves or their neighbor. Brian swallowed but only said, "Yeah, got it. Watch your step."

Presently, they noticed that the light in the tunnel was increasing and it looked like they were nearing the exit to the tunnel. Raneous stopped with nostrils flared and ears twitching back and forth listening and trying to sense if there was danger up ahead. All seemed clear.

"I half expected to meet an evil welcome party at this end of the tunnel." he noted.

"The idea had occurred to me too!" Mick confirmed.

The light got brighter and the entrance was just ahead. Brian started to rush eagerly ahead anxious to be away from guano and creepers but Mick held him back. "Wait, let's be cautious and wary. We know we have an enemy so let's be smart about this."

"Right." Brian felt a little foolish but buried his hand in Raneous' mane taking comfort in the stallion's strength as they walked cautiously forward together to the mouth of the tunnel wondering anxiously what might be awaiting them.

11- AN ANGEL, A GIRL

They reached the entrance together, and there they stood and took in the beautiful view of the valley below.

"Look! There's Livia!" Mick pointed over to the right. "So, I guess the gypsy woman gave us some truth. We may never know what her real motives were."

They were fairly high up and could see the valley below full of fruit orchards, farmland and gentle rolling hills. To the right was the beautiful city of Livia surrounded by a thick stone wall with great iron gates placed strategically at four corners. Right in the center was a tall and ancient but beautiful castle flashing golden in the sun. The windows of its tall towers caught the sun's rays so the whole castle seemed to sparkle and twinkle like a diamond.

"Wow!" Brian caught his breath. He had never seen a city so beautiful.

"My home!" Mick smiled with pride. "Beautiful Livia! The crown jewel of the East!" Mick's voice caught in his throat. "But she is sick, and chaos and division are tearing her apart."

As they all took in the view, Raneous caught a glimmer out of the corner of his eye and turned to look. Standing on one of the lower branches of a tall pine tree was an angel!

"Shhh! Only you can see and hear me, Raneous." The words lit upon Raneous' mind even as he saw the angel speak. The angel was a warrior, for a powerful sword was slung at his side, and a shield hung over his back, but his eyes twinkled at Raneous. *"You have done well, my friend! I am Kiran. Your praise not only gave you your wings but opened the way for me to drive back the demonic forces surrounding you. Your way is clear to Livia!"* Kiran's face became solemn, *"The demon, Murmul, and his vermin are plotting against you and you must use the King's wisdom and guidance once in Livia. There is a battle brewing. Look and see the dark clouds that gather in the East and the North."* Raneous looked and indeed the dark churning clouds were growing and creeping over the mountain tops inching their way toward the city. *"But be of good courage for the High King, the Captain of the Host, is strong and true!"* And the angel was gone.

Raneous blinked and looked around searching, but there was no sign of Kiran or any other heavenly beings. In spite of the abrupt departure, his heart lifted with the knowledge that they had made some headway in this battle, and he had seen one of the Heavenly Host.

"The way is clear until we get to Livia!" Raneous announced with certainty.

Mick and Brian looked at the horse in surprise. "You seem pretty certain of that." Mick looked curiously at Raneous.

Raneous then told them about the angel and what he had told him about their praise in the tunnel and how it had cleared their way. Something kept him from telling them about the coming storm - at least for now. He had learned that the Shadowlanders cannot see the demonic storm clouds as he could.

"Well! If that doesn't beat all!" Mick exclaimed. "Traveling with you brings a whole new dimension to things, I see."

Brian was disappointed that he didn't see the angel too. "Why did he hide himself from us? I've seen demons before, why can't I see an angel?"

"I don't know, Brian, but he didn't stay long and he may have been in a hurry." Raneous puzzled. "At any rate, we can move quickly now knowing we won't be held up."

Down the winding path they went, descending into the valley and the trees. The sight of Livia disappeared behind the pines, but Mick knew where they were. Presently, they came to another very large and very overgrown hedge blocking the ancient path.

"I would bet that the main road is just on the other side of this hedge. I would give my supper to know the story behind this mysterious path and why it is so thoroughly blocked off from use!" Mick pondered as he studied the large hedge. "I'll push through and see what I find."

Like the first hedge, it was not impossible to push through, and sure enough, Mick stepped out only a few feet from the main road to Livia. The other two joined him quickly and at last they were nearing their destination.

"Brian, up on my back! We need to look like normal travelers." the horse directed.

Brian caught a glimpse of the castle's highest tower through the trees. "We are getting close. Do we have a plan? Do we know what we are going to do once we arrive?" Brian realized they had been so focused on just getting to Livia, that now that they were here, what were they actually going to do?" This set his heart beating a little faster than he cared to admit.

Mick hesitated, "I think we should not go through the Western Gate since we might be expected there. Let's travel around to the Southern Gate – it's less traveled anyway and I live on the south side of Livia. We can go to my home and flesh out a plan from there." Mick eyed Raneous. "You're just so majestic! Someone like me could never afford a horse like you. We need to cover some of you up!"

Brian dismounted and quickly pulled out their blankets from their tent roll. He spread his mother's handmade quilt over Raneous' powerful back and stepped back to see the affect. "Well, it doesn't make you look any smaller, but you do look a little less…white!" He said hopefully.

"It will have to do for now." Mick chewed his lip nervously wondering what plan they could come up with. *"Well, High King, I hope you have a plan! I'm just a musician, not a magician!"*

"I hope you have a stable or barn or something. I'm not going to fit very well through the front door of your house." Raneous winked at Mick.

"Yes," Mick chuckled, "It's not much, but yes I do."
More travelers were on the road with carts and horses or mules loaded with goods heading for the market. The three spoke less as they didn't want to draw attention to themselves. They were now nearing the Western Gate.

"We are going right at the fork and that will take us to the Southern Gate." Mick said softly.

As they approached the Western Gate, the road filled with people. In spite of Raneous' quilt, he was attracting quite a few stares, but no one questioned them. Everyone seemed to be preoccupied with their own problems. It struck Raneous that he did not see one happy face! Frowns, scowls and unhappy mumblings caught his sharp ears. Mick was right! Beautiful Livia was not a happy place these days! Raneous looked at the rich farmland, and the fruitful orchards. *"What was everyone so unhappy about? Could rats really be that bad? Well, rats and snakes actually. Everyone is decidedly grumpy!"*

"They have lost My joy."

"High King, how do you fight joylessness?"

"Try to plod along, will you? Don't carry your head so high!" Mick muttered out of the corner of his mouth.

Raneous dutifully tried to droop and look stupid. In spite of the tension Brian was feeling, this made him want to laugh, but he held it in with effort.

As most of the crowd was using the Western Gate, the crowd thinned out again as they moved around to the right with Livia's stone wall on their left. But the three travelers could hear shouts coming from inside the city like a big crowd had gathered. They were chanting something. The words became recognizable as they strained to hear.

"DOWN WITH KING JERALD! DOWN WITH KING JERALD!"

Mick gave a low whistle, "Whew! Things have gotten worse since I left! The city sounds like it's in an uproar!"

They walked on in silence listening to the chaos within the city walls and wondering what they could possibly do to help such a complicated mess. It seemed to take forever, but just as they were nearing the Southern Gate, Brian noticed a girl about his age watching them intently by the side of the road. Her large gray eyes followed them closely.

"*She's really pretty.*" Brian suddenly blushed and looked away, a little alarmed at the direction of his thoughts.

The girl seemed to make up her mind about them. Carrying a basket of apples over one arm, she approached Mick. As Brian watched her, he noticed that she was petite and moved with a lightness he had never seen in any other girl he knew. But then, he didn't know too many. He did notice that her shiny, dark brown hair reached past her waist in one long braid and that her grey eyes were fringed with long thick lashes. Brian gulped and looked away trying to focus on something – anything- else.

Luckily for Brian, the girl was focused on Mick so she missed Brian's embarrassing discomfort.

"You are the man Anna the Prophetess met in the square more than a week ago, are you not?" The girl looked steadily at Mick but also glanced over at the large white stallion. Brian saw admiration light up her face as she took in the regal animal – in spite of the quilt.

Mick started, but answered readily, seeing this as a sign, "Yes, I am. Who are you?"

"I'm Roslyn, and you must come with me and not go into the city right now. You are to follow me to the prophetess' house. She was given a message by the High King to meet you here at the Southern Gate today. She said that you would be traveling with a white horse and a boy." At this, Roslyn glanced up at Brian and gave him an ever-so-slight smile before looking back at Mick.

Brian's heart leaped up and began racing madly around inside his chest. He took deep breaths trying to calm himself. *What is wrong with me?!*

"Oh!" Roslyn started in surprise. Raneous, who had gently grabbed her sleeve with his teeth, was drawing in deep, yearning breaths of the sweet smelling apples that she was carrying.

Mick laughed, "Raneous is all about the food!"

Roslyn laughed and picked an apple for the hungry horse and gave Mick and Brian one too. Their fingers brushed as Brian took the apple from her and the light touch set his heart pounding wildly in his ears again just as it had finally settled down.

"Just stop it!" he said to himself.

"Anna will have supper waiting for us, I think. Her cottage is about an hour's walk from here if we take this path that's here off to the right." Roslyn pointed to a small dirt road leading into the fields and woods. She was completely unaware of the panic she was causing in the boy seated above her.

Mick's stomach growled noisily. "I guess we would all be happy to get some food!" he laughed, holding his stomach.

With the thoughts of hot food in their near future, the group set off willingly with their new friend hoping that their way would be made clear in their unknown mission.

High on the city walls, in a deserted guard tower, a large black rat observed the meeting down below. Word had been sent from Murmel's demon assistant to look for travelers with a white horse and to track their movements. The rat turned, "Go vermin, and discover what you can! Report back to me what you learn!" Ten rats skittered silently over the wall, across the road, and into the woods, out of sight behind the unaware travelers.

12- THE TWINS

The path that the travelers had taken proved a pleasant one as they walked away from the chaotic noise of the city and into the shaded trees of the forest.

"So how do you know this prophetess, Anna? You're too old to be her daughter, I think" Mick asked sociably.

"She is my aunt, my mother's youngest sister. My twin brother and I are staying with her because of everything going on in the city." Roslyn sighed, "I really miss the city! I miss the music and the dance!"

"The dance?" Brian finally found his tongue.

"My parents are the directors of the Livia Theater and School of Fine Arts. I love the dance. It is my life. My brother loves acting and acrobatics – he's the daredevil of the family!"

"Wow!" Brian swallowed. Talented, pretty and way over his head! He felt small and insignificant next to this artful creature.

The girl glanced up at Brian, "What does your family do?"

"Well…" Brian thought of all the hard work they had put into their farm to bring it back to life. He thought of his mom baking and sewing and making butter to sell at the market. He thought of milking cows, sheering sheep and feeding chickens.

"We're farmers. We grow and make all kinds of things." Brian felt there were not enough words to describe what all they did, and that it would sound very dull.

Mick laughed, "They're great people and skilled at their work! Their farm was the best looking one I had come across in my search for the white horse! The Borderlands are a tough place to farm and they have done nothing short of a miracle to accomplish what they have."

Brian flashed Mick a grateful look and sat up a little straighter in his saddle.

"Wow! I know nothing about farming, though I am learning about apple orchards being with Auntie Anna. But it sounds amazing!" Roslyn flashed a smile up to Brian.

Brian blushed and looked quickly away. Mick caught the look and chuckled to himself, *"Ah, thirteen and discovering girls! This ought to be fun!"* "Why Brian! Was that…" Luckily for Brian, he never got to finish.

"HEY! HO! Look alive!" A cheerful call seemed to be coming from up in the trees somewhere.

The party looked up in surprise and saw a youth balancing on a tight rope that was strung between two tall trees high over the path. In his hands was a large pole to aid in his balance. He was swaying slightly but grinning down at them as he completed the crossing to the safety of the supporting tree.

"Rhyse! Auntie is going to kill you!" Roslyn, having dropped her apples in surprise, had her hands on her hips in that "mother" attitude. "You know she doesn't like you doing acrobatics like this! There's no net! No safety wires!"

Rhyse, having reached the trees safely, did not answer but quickly swung down and dropped dramatically in front of them with a bow. "Rhyse at your service!"

Brian couldn't help but laugh and instantly liked this boy's cocky confidence. Rhyse was about Brian's height with black curly hair, light olive skin, and of all things, goldish eyes. Brian looked again but the gold color was unmistakable in his tanned face.

"What Auntie doesn't know won't hurt her! And she wanted me to watch for you, but sitting and doing nothing is boring, so I have been entertaining myself, the birds, and the squirrels. I have to keep my skills sharp even if I have been banished to the far country!"

Roslyn rolled her eyes and gave Mick and Brian an apologizing look. "This is my twin, Rhyse, in case you haven't guessed." Roslyn then made the introductions around.

"Wow! Auntie Anna doesn't miss much does she? I mean, she said look for a man traveling with a white horse and a boy and here you are! Unbelievable!" Rhyse stood grinning at them all.

"Miracles happen when you serve the High King." Raneous commented matter of factly with a nod of his regal head.

"Look who's talking! Why, you ARE a miracle in my book! A talking horse – and I hear you fly too! Rhyse looked at Raneous with a mixture of joy and wonderment on his face.

Brain smiled. Anyone who thought Raneous was wonderful was okay in his book. He still pinched himself sometimes to make sure he was awake and Raneous was really back with him. A shiver of joy went through his soul. Whatever happens, as long as Raneous was there Brian believed he could take on anything.

"Come on! I know Auntie Anna is cooking up some chicken and potatoes for us. But even better is the homemade apple pie!" With that Rhyse did a back hand spring landing beautifully on his feet.

Mick laughed, "You're not one to stand still for very long are you?"

Rhyse grinned back at them, "Why walk when you can do a cartwheel instead? Besides, I'm hungry and I'll bet you are too!"

Brian's stomach growled loudly in response. Mick laughed, "Heaven forbid we keep hungry teenage boys from their food! But today I'm right with them!"

Auntie Anna's cottage was snuggly surrounded by large oak trees, but Brian could see and smell the apple orchards off to the right. Her house was a small cottage with a thatched roof, shuttered windows and also a loft by the look of the open window near the roof's peak. Standing in the doorway was the prophetess waving cheerily to them. Brian, now agreed with Mick that she was definitely too young to be the twins' parent. Long, curly, strawberry blonde hair hung down her back tied loosely with a black ribbon. But as they neared, Brian noticed that her face, though youthful, had an underlying seriousness to it. Brian was reminded that Auntie Anna was also Anna the Prophetess.

"You have come! The High King be praised!" Anna's smile included them all but her blue eyes were fixed on Raneous.

"The High King sent me, but to be honest I do not know the plan." Raneous bowed his head to the young woman in greeting.

"I believe that is why He sent you to me. We are to make plans under his guidance and in a place that the enemy cannot get in." Anna looked around at them all. "I know you have had to fight to get here, so now we will call upon the High King's Ring of Fire because I am sure you have been followed."

"Yes, I have sensed an evil close, but not too close." The stallion confirmed with a snort and a flare of his nostrils.

Mick and Brian looked at each other in surprise, as Raneous had said nothing of it earlier.

"Then I will waste no time. She picked up a stout walking stick that was leaning against a rough wooden table. "I moved our table outside so our horse friend can be included in our talks." Anna winked at Raneous.

This won't take long and then we can eat!" Anna proceeded to step out past the travelers about fifty feet and drew a line in the dirt path.

"High King, I ask that you send a ring of fire to encircle this property that no dark force can come past this line. This property belongs to your servant and therefore it belongs to you, and all who enter are protected." Anna turned right and continued to drag the stick on the ground saying, "A ring of fire, O King. A ring of fire for your servants."

The travelers watched her curiously as she made her way around the back of her property to complete a full circle. "There!" Anna looked up and smiled at the puzzled party as she connected the line in the dirt. "That will do it."

Brian glanced sideways at Mick, who shrugged his shoulders in response. Nothing seemed different to Mick. A circle in the dirt around her property didn't seem like any kind of protection to him. But Brian gasped in wonder, for as Anna walked, he saw orange tongues of fire leap up from the ground along her dirt line. But even more amazing was every ten feet or so a very large angel materialized with a flaming sword held high. Brian could see their massive backs and shoulders as they faced outwards, warding off anything that would try to invade them. So when Anna finished her circle, there were twelve fifteen- foot angels with flaming swords encircling Anna's property.

"Raneous! I see them! I see them!" Brian whispered excitedly.

"The High King has answered your prayer, Brian. You have seen angels." Raneous responded with a soft whicker.

Mick, Roslyn and Rhyse did not see anything but took the other's word for it, though they were disappointed.

"Well, I feel safe!" Rhyse announced. "Now let's eat! My stomach is starting to chew on itself!"

Outside the angelic flames, ten very angry and frustrated rats hissed and spat uselessly but they could neither see nor hear anything from inside the ring of fire.

"We're rat stew for sure! Curse that prophetess!"

"Silence!" the largest of the rats ordered. "We wait. They can't stay in there forever. We wait and watch."

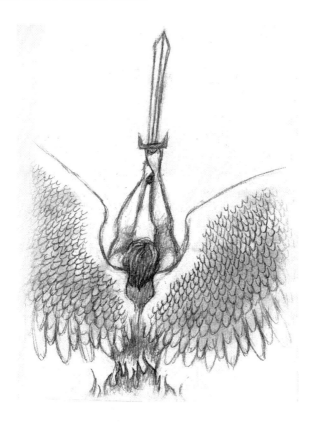

13- THE PLAN

It was a beautiful morning and Brian breathed deeply of the fresh, cool morning breeze that tasseled his brown, wavy hair. Now, they were all planning to head for Livia. All, that is, except Anna. Brian thought about last night and tried to keep his anxious thoughts in check about what they were up against. *"We serve the High King. He will help us. Please, let me be brave enough!"* The last thought was a silent plea. He really liked his new friends, but he felt small and insignificant next to their confidence and talents.

"Remember they were looking for a horse AND a rider.."

This thought lit gently on his mind and Brian's spirit lifted. He had a part to play in this – they all did- and each part was important. He thought of their dinner last night safe inside their angelic guard. He had never felt so safe eating under the stars with these new friends who were so willing to help. As they ate, they had talked about possible ways to find Sam but nothing seemed right. Anna had listened intently to everything saying nothing, but her blues eyes searched their faces thoughtfully. Then when the meal was finished, she quietly pulled a scroll out of her apron pocket, unrolled it on the table, and proceeded to read it to them by the light of the lantern. She read the following:

Attention Citizens of the Eastern Region!

His Most Excellent Highness, King Jerald of Livia and the Eastern Region, has hereby decreed that all fit stallions and geldings with their owners report to the King's Captain of the Guard at the royal stables for inspection. If the horse and owner are found worthy of duty, the owner and the horse will be sworn into the service of the king for one year. If the horse is found worthy but the owner unfit, a fair price will be made for the horse and the owner will relinquish his ownership of the said horse to the king's stables. This decree becomes effective immediately. Those who refuse to comply will be subject to imprisonment.

"I saw the palace guards posting these around the city while I was at the market early this morning. Apparently, King Jerald is feeling the need to reinforce his mounted guard." Anna looked around the table and then smiled. Brian noticed she had dimples.

"We are centered in the High King's perfect timing! This is how we will get into the palace! And it's also why Raneous was not supposed to go into the city today before we laid our plans!"

Mick laughed and slapped his knee, "Yes! We have the perfect horse!"

Everyone agreed that this was certainly an amazing development. But Brian was puzzled.

"How do we know we have to get into the palace? Sam could be anywhere!"

All eyes turned back to Anna. "Well, I wouldn't have known except early this morning I got a message from a dear friend of mine who is a cook in the castle. She had sent the message by way of her small son because she was afraid to write it down. She had him memorize it-and a long one it was-poor little guy. The message from Essie was that she had gone to take the breakfast leftovers to the pigs kept out in back of the castle. She doesn't normally do this, but the servant girl had twisted her ankle, so she offered to do it for her.

The castle is somewhat confusing and she ended up taking a wrong turn. Just as she realized her mistake and was turning back, she saw Queen Vanora. Essie ducked inside a door frame and watched her. The queen was alone. Not even the nasty snake she seemed to love was with her and she was acting strangely...looking around to see if anyone was watching and tip toeing. She slipped through a back door and out of the castle. Essie, full of burning curiosity, abandoned her pig slop and carefully followed the queen at a distance. The queen headed to the castle cemetery and stopped at the door of a very large and ancient crypt. Again, the queen looked around carefully. Then she faced the crypt door and presented her right hand to it. A large, red- eyed python snake dropped down and examined her hand. Essie said that she saw red light pass from the serpent ring on the queen's hand to the red eyes of the python. Then the door of the crypt opened and the queen entered with the door shutting noiselessly behind her."

Anna looked excitedly around at her spellbound audience. "So the ring is like a key or a pass to enter the crypt!"

Mick's eyes were wide in open admiration, "Anna, you are a most amazing woman! I would bet supper for a year that is where my brother and maybe many others are being held captive. Though honestly the problem is we still don't know why, and getting a ring off of Queen Vanora's hand sounds nearly impossible. So, what now?"

Roslyn and Rhyse looked at each other and said in unison, "The King's birthday is tomorrow!"

Roslyn continued excitedly, "If we had not been sent to Auntie Anna's we would have both been in the performance at the palace tomorrow night! The dancers' changing rooms are not far from the queen's chambers. Since I actually helped with the choreography, no one would think it odd if I was there – except my mother, of course." She finished with a grimace and a pleading glance to her aunt.

And so they had talked late into the night working out the details of who was doing what and now Brian, Raneous, Mick, Roslyn and Rhyse were heading back to Livia, each with a part to be played out in its time.

Anna had spent much of the night sending out messages by carrier pigeons to her various sources requesting the proper clothes and harnesses for Mick, Brian and Raneous. Her sister, the twins' mother, ended up being the biggest help. Anna had also sent word to her telling her it was of a most urgent matter that Roslyn be allowed in the castle during the king's birthday performance. Though her sister didn't know the mission, she trusted Anna and had also graciously supplied the livery clothes and nobleman's clothes from her theater's costume department. Brian fingered the buttons on his new livery uniform. A beautiful black and silver saddle and bridle outfit had mysteriously been delivered by an unknown donor early this morning - at least unknown to everyone except Anna, who had just smiled and said nothing. Mick was now dressed out in a beautiful black feathered hat, cloak and high leather riding boots. Gone was his traveler's scruffy beard and in its place was a clean shaven chin and a magnificent handlebar mustache secured tightly with costume glue. Raneous jingled majestically in his new finery, the black and silver a beautiful contrast with his white coat. Now hopefully, with the High King's help, they would succeed in finding Sam.

14- THE KING'S STABLES

The Southern Gate was up ahead. Mick raised his arm, "Stop here." He turned and looked around at them. "This is where we must separate. Raneous, Brian and I will continue through the Southern Gate while you twins would do better to go back to the Western Gate so that we are not seen entering the city together."

The twins looked at each other solemnly, their eyes a little wider than normal at the thought of what they were about to do. But suddenly, Rhyse grinned at them all, "This will be great fun! See you soon!" And off the two went.

Mick chuckled as they walked quickly away, "Gotta love that kind of confidence." Then he turned to Brian who was riding Raneous. "Now it's time for you to switch with me. I am now the young nobleman and you are the stable boy from here on out. The weird thing about this is that I may end up being in the king's mounted guard for a year because of what we're doing."

Brian quickly dismounted. "Okay Raneous, from here on you need to keep your words to yourself. Just normal horse noises."

Raneous tossed his head and snorted but said nothing. Mick grinned as he mounted up. "To the king's stables we go."

*

The royal stables were bustling with activity. Men of all ages were making their way to be inspected and they were not happy about it.

"Who does King Jerald think he is taking my horse- or me for that matter? Since when did we become slaves without any say in our future? I have a business to run and I need my horse!"

The Captain of the Guard, a powerful man with a thick, red beard and piercing blue eyes was in a foul mood as he busily took down names standing on the back of a wagon. In front of the wagon, his aid directed traffic.

"To the right there! To the right! Once you've stated your name, move to the right!" The flustered aid yelled over the noise of the crowd.

Brian held tightly to Raneous' bridle as he was jostled and bumped by the crowd of angry men and their nervous horses. One man began arguing loudly with the Captain of the Guard, shaking his fist threateningly in the Captain's face. This proved a huge mistake.

The Captain, his face red with anger, drew his sword and jumped off the wagon. He grabbed the startled man by the shoulder and spun him around laying the blade of his sword across the now terrified man's neck.

"I'll show you who's boss here!" the Captain shouted into the man's ear. "Guards! Take him to the stocks where he can think about his shameful behavior. Take his horse! It now belongs to the king – free of charge!"

The now humiliated man was led quickly away by the guards. This scene had an amazingly quieting affect on the crowd. A spirit of cooperation emerged and everyone began to line up in order to patiently wait their turn. No one dared to say anything cross to anyone. Brian and Mick exchanged looks but remained silent.

"Name?"

It was their turn. Mick gulped but said with confidence, "Mitchell of Greensboro, sir."

The Captain was scribbling fiercely on his tablet and barely looked up, but did a double take when he saw the white stallion in front of him. His eyes followed the lines of the stallion with expertise. He looked at Mick with a new interest.

"Greensboro? I'm not familiar with it. We just sent out the couriers this morning with the proclamation." He eyed Mick curiously.

"Well sir, I happened to be in town and saw the postings here in the market. Greensboro is a small little known burg on the far western borders of King Jerald's region." Mick hoped this was an intelligent answer.

"We should know more about it if you grow horses like this." The Captain, in spite of the long line waiting, ran his hand over Raneous' withers and checked his teeth.

"Yes, well, this horse was my inheritance from my late uncle, so unfortunately he is the only one in Greensboro." Mick cleared his throat and studied his hands thoughtfully.

"A pity, but I believe King Jerald will want to see you and your horse personally. I see you have a stable boy." The Captain of the Guard clapped his massive hands together, "Tom!"

A youth, a little older than Brian, appeared by the Captain's side. "Here, sir." The boy bowed slightly.

"Take this gentleman and this horse and his stable boy to the king's stable. Make them comfortable. Then send word to the king that there is a horse worthy of his immediate inspection."

The boy bowed again and motioned for Mick and Brian to follow him.

Brian suddenly had a horrible thought. *What if the king took Raneous from them?* A cold chill went through his body. *Could the king do that? Of course he could, but the king did not know that Raneous was a free being owned by no one. I wonder if Raneous has thought about this?* Brian took a deep breath to steady his nerves. Well, they were in it now and all they could do was move forward and see how it unfolded. Brian caught a movement out of the corner of his eye. Something dark was hiding in the shadow of the castle wall. Brian caught his breath again. A rat! A huge rat was watching them! It met Brian's eye and just like that it disappeared. They were being watched. Brian noticed Raneous's nostrils flare and realized he had seen it too. The stallion stayed calm, but Brian felt a tremor go through the horse and he understood that Raneous was holding himself back with great effort. Even Raneous has to pick his battles, and now was not the time to reveal his true identity. Timing was everything here. They were going to be in the king's stable the night of the birthday celebration and that was exactly what they had hoped for. The king's stables were massive and had the ability to house hundreds of horses. They were clean, well ventilated, and best of all, situated behind the castle and were an easy distance from the cemetery. *"I hope Rhyse and Roslyn can get to their posts in time."* Their parts in this seemed the most dangerous to him. Brian shuddered to think what would happen to them or even their parents if they were caught.

"Here you are." Tom, the messenger boy, indicated a nice clean stall with a jerk of his head. They had entered the stables while Brian was deep in thought. "There's a bunk room off to your left. You and your boy can rest there for now while I send word to Her Highness…I mean His Highness." The boy smiled awkwardly and then left.

They waited until they heard the wooden door click shut and they all drew a collective sigh of relief. They were alone except for some other horses in neighboring stalls. Raneous put his head in his trough to sample the fresh hay. Brian sat down in the stall beside him.

"I saw that rat, Raneous! Do you think they know what we are up to?"

Raneous shook his head as he munched and slowly winked his eye, remembering not to speak.

Mick overheard the question and said, "They can't know what we are doing, but they know we are doing something. So keep it quiet. We are going to be seeing the king soon. Brian, keep the hay and dirt off of you and remember your part. We want to be able to stay here tonight." Luckily for them, Anna had thought to pack them some bread, dried beef and apples. So they settled down to wait for their inspection.

"Play us a tune, Mick. Something calm." Brian said, his head leaning against the stall and staring at the roof.

Mick happily obliged, pulling out his flute pouch and selecting his wooden flute. Brian closed his eyes and let the soft, low notes soothe his anxious spirit.

"Whatever happens, High King, we are in your hands."

While Mick played, the stable doors opened and in walked a stable boy leading a magnificent dark red horse.

15- FEEDING ON DIRT

Roslyn and Rhyse made their way through the crowded Western Gate with all the other Livians who were bringing their produce to market, or as a result of the king's newest proclamation, their horse to the king's stables. Roslyn, noticing a lot of very unhappy and angry faces, stuck close to her brother as they ducked in and out of the crowd. They knew this city like the backs of their hands so as soon as possible, Rhyse slipped into a back alley where they could catch their breath. The problem was that these days the back alleys were also infested with rats and snakes crawling in and out of drain pipes and garbage bins so their rest was brief.

As they ran swiftly through the narrow alleys of Livia, they came upon a group of three women washing clothes. They had their hair all tied back in handkerchiefs and their sleeves rolled up. However, the dirty laundry lay piled around their feet untouched and the waiting soapy water in the wash tub ignored. Their hands were idle but their tongues were not. Rhyse slowed to pass quietly by them, so the twins were able to hear the women's conversation. And by the looks on their faces it was a matter of high interest.

"King Jerald is all washed up, I say! He's going downhill bad. Why, Queen Vanora is at her wits end and is having to take on many of his duties. Poor thing! She had no idea when she married him he was on the brink of insanity!"

"Yes, it's a shame!" the second woman nodded knowingly. "Have you seen his eyes lately? Shifty. He can't be trusted, I tell you. We're all going to come to a bad end if he's allowed to stay in power!"

The third woman chimed in, "And now this ridiculous demand on our horses! The king's afraid! I would bet my life on it!"

The first woman shook her head, "No, he's always been brainless. We are just now wising up to his stupidity." She spat the last word with venom. On and on they talked. They were just getting warmed up.

Roslyn felt suddenly saddened and disgusted by it. It was like they wanted King Jerald to go insane or the whole city to fall apart. As they quietly moved passed the women – who took no notice of them – Roslyn caught movement in one of the piles of dirty laundry. Roslyn gasped, but swallowed her squeal before it escaped her lips.

It was a python snake! It was at least eight to ten inches thick. Roslyn could see the giant coils underneath the pile of clothes as they lay on the dusty, dirty street. It seemed to be coiling tighter, for the clothes were shifting. It stretched out and flicked its tongue at the feet of one of the women. Roslyn grabbed Rhyse's hand to halt him. They both stopped and then watched in horror at the scene that was unfolding before them.

Each of the women had a pile of laundry at her feet. As the women continued to cut down their leader, their city, and all they could think of, the twins noticed the other piles of laundry starting to shift. Suddenly, as if on cue, huge coils shot out from under all three clothes piles and wrapped themselves around the women's waists, binding their arms fast to their sides. They all shrieked in terror but only once. The snakes coils tightened on their chests, causing them to be unable to draw enough breath to scream. Coil after coil the snakes quickly wound them up. The three women could not move, and their eyes bugged out from the pressure and the terror.

"Quick! Find a stick – anything to beat them off of them!" Rhyse yelled as he ran to the closest victim and began beating the coils of the snake with his balance rod.

"WHACK!!" Rhyse hit the coils of the snake as hard as he could. The snake's head turned to him in a fury and hissed. To Rhyse's surprise he heard words!

"She's mine by right! She has spoken! I feed on her dust! I feed on her dirt!"

WHAM!! Roslyn had found a broom and was using it on a second snake, but it wasn't working either. Even as they beat on the coils, yelling at the snakes to let the women go, the snakes were slithering and dragging their victims to an open manhole in the alley. Roslyn wasn't sure how a coiled snake and its victim would fit, but it was like it could shrink itself and its victim to fit the opening. The first snake disappeared down the dark hole with Rhyse beating on it even as it disappeared.

"NO! NO!" Roslyn screamed in desperation at the last disappearing snake. She burst out crying. "Oh, how awful! What will happen to them?" Roslyn covered her face trying to erase the horrible scene from her memory. Rhyse was trembling but grimly put his arm around his sister as he stared at the empty manhole in the street.

"Gone! If I had not seen it, I would not have believed any of it!" Rhyse said in a hushed tone as he stared around at the now abandoned wash.

"Don't you see?" Roslyn looked up at him with a tear streaked face. "We just witnessed a disappearance! This explains a lot. You can see why nobody knows anything – it happens so fast and with so little noise."

"Did you hear that snake? Somehow it has some kind of right to its victims." Rhyse looked at his balancing pole he was still holding. "And I couldn't do a thing about it!"

Roslyn's large gray eyes grew even larger as a thought hit her. "Do you think that how they were talking about King Jerald had anything to do with it? I mean, they were being very… I don't know… negative and mean!"

"'I feed on her dirt.' The snake said. Maybe that's what it meant." Rhyse frowned in thought, but Rhyse was not one to be still for long, so since nothing else could be done at this point, his face cleared and he shook himself. "Well, we best keep moving, because I think the best way to help those women and any others is to continue on our mission. Let's go, sis."

Reluctantly, Roslyn agreed, but her heart ached and shuddered for the terror those women must be feeling, if they were even still alive. She and her brother needed to stay focused.

*

The twins were nearing the castle. As they passed through the market square, they saw people busily preparing for the royal birthday. Garlands of fresh flowers were strung between buildings. The Livian flag hung from many second story windows, and bakers and merchants were preparing their tables and setting up tents. Roslyn was struck by how different it felt than last year. Livians love to celebrate and they do it well. Usually, everyone is in high spirits laughing and joking as they work to make the celebration a good one. This year Roslyn could sense a tension in the air. Everything looked good on the surface but the faces of the people were reserved. Some even looked resentful as they went about their preparations.

"Oh Rhyse!" Roslyn whispered. "Our beautiful Livia is sick!"

Rhyse squeezed her hand but said nothing. "Look!" He pointed across the square. "There's our dance company! We're right on time!"

There was no need for them to be cautious at this point. It was the most natural thing for them to be a part of this group. Roslyn spotted her mother surrounded by a cluster of acrobats. She was busily going over the checklist for props and costumes. Her mother's light brown hair was pulled back in a classic bun with a ring of small flowers circling her brow. Her face was full of that before-the-big-performance worry as people from all sides pressed in upon her.

"Ms. Tabitha! Here are the tambourines you requested."

"Ms. Tabitha, I have a run in my tights, I must go change!"

"I lost my gloves!"

All would be put right in Ms. Tabitha's capable hands, but the twins wisely blended in with the rest of the performers and left their mother alone.

"Here comes Papa!" Roslyn pointed to a strong looking figure on the back of a dapple gray mare coming towards them. Roslyn loved her papa's dark good looks. It was a look uncommon to this region, for their father was a native of the Southern Islands. She and Rhyse had both inherited his light olive skin tone, but Rhyse had also gotten his father's unusual golden eyes and dark, loose curls.

"Everyone in your places please!" Myran, the twins' father, quieted the group. "The queen has graciously let us come in early so that we will have time to set up and run through some routines before the banquet tonight."

Sighs of relief went through the performers and smiles appeared. "Leave it to Mr. Myran. He can work his magic on anybody! He's the best!" one acrobat whispered to Rhyse. Apparently, Queen Vanora had been opposed to letting in the performers before the actual time of the banquet. And also apparently, the twins' father had successfully been able to help her understand the need for it.

So with Myran on his dapple gray mare leading the procession, they made their way from the market square to the main gates of the castle. The twins were dead last in the procession, and just before they passed through the huge stone arches, Rhyse winked at Roslyn and said, "This is where I get off!" Balance pole in hand, he slipped into a dark side hallway and disappeared.

16- THE KING'S INTERVIEW

"Wow, sir!" the stable boy said to Mick. "Don't quit your playin' on my account! You have a magical touch to that pipe."

Mick smiled, "Thanks…" Mick eyed the large red horse. "I see you brought another candidate for the king's inspection."

The boy grinned as he patted the beautiful red head. Surprisingly, the animal flinched at his touch. "That gypsy woman was furious to have to give him up! Threatened to put a curse on the king. She's a bit scary. Said something about having friends in dark places and she had earned the right to that horse."

Something clicked in Brian's mind. "Hey, was she wearing a peacock feather hat and lots of beads?"

The stable boy looked at Brian for the first time. "Oh, didn't see you there. Uh…yeah she was, actually. You know her?"

Mick shot Brian a warning look and answered, "Well no, we just saw her on the road here is all."

Raneous suddenly stomped his foot and tossing his head, gave a sharp whinny. The two stallions had locked eyes. The red horse, nostrils flared answered in kind. With great effort, the stable boy kept hold of his lead rope.

"Stallions! They are so hot blooded! Always wanting to fight!" the stable boy said through gritted teeth as he strained to keep the red horse in check. "Keep these two separated, for sure!"

The large wooden doors at the end of the stable opened as two guards hurriedly took their places.

"Quick! Everyone at attention! Bring the horses out of their stalls but give 'em space! The king is here!" the flustered boy took a firmer grip on the red horse and guided him out to stand for the king. Brian followed his example and led Raneous to stand as well. Raneous immediately calmed down and stood quietly.

Mick removed his hat, smoothed his hair, and took a deep breath. *"Here we go!"*

"King Jerald and Queen Vanora!" the herald proclaimed as the royal couple stepped into the stable.

A cold chill ran down Mick's spine as the king came into view. The king had aged alarmingly! His skin looked thin and had a yellowish cast to it. His eyes were rimmed in red as they darted around the room and in their depths Mick saw fear. King Jerald was leaning heavily on his queen's arm, who by contrast, looked more beautiful than ever with her long, raven black hair coiled around her head in an elaborate braided crown. With her free hand, she patted her husband's hand reassuringly. Mick caught the sparkle of the ruby eyes of her serpent ring. Mick quickly looked away before his face betrayed his feelings.

"Ah, my dear king, these are truly beautiful animals, are they not?" Queen Vanora gently directed the king's gaze to the red and the white horses. Her voice was sweet but her eyes were cold and calculating as she considered these prizes. "There is no rider for the red horse?"

The stable boy bowed, "The owner is a gypsy woman, Your Majesty."

"Well, a gypsy has no business with a horse of this beauty and strength. He will be put to much better use as part of the King's Guard!" The queen paused to consider, "But of course we will give her a fair price – though I warrant she stole him! Stable boy, I assign you personally to this horse…does it have a name?"

"The woman called him Horse, Your Majesty."

"So unbelievably uncreative! No matter, we will get him civilized and properly named, I'm sure. Now my king, come and let us look at this white beauty!" Queen Vanora, along with the king, approached Raneous, Mick and Brian. "Well, it is easy to see this horse has plenty of support – even a stable boy! And you are Mitchell of Greensboro?"

"Why yes, your Majesty, I am." Mick answered in surprise.

Queen Vanora smiled, "I make it a point to know my subjects —our subjects." She corrected. "He was your inheritance, was he not? You were here on business when you saw the proclamation and so you came immediately. That was very…honest of you." The queen looked curiously at Mick. True loyalty was rare and he might become very useful.

"Oh my!" the queen started in surprise. Raneous had suddenly stepped forward and had gently placed his head under King Jerald's limp hand. As he gently raised his regal head, he looked into the king's troubled eyes and softly nickered.

"Don't mind Raneous. He loves people your Majesty." Mick reassured the queen but privately wondered what the stallion was up to.

The king, with his hand still on Raneous's forehead, slowly smiled as his troubled eyes focused on the intelligent and gentle eyes looking into his own. Slowly he spoke, "This one! This one is for me. He will protect me." The king stood there and stroked the large white head with a look of peace on his lined face. As Brian quietly watched, he thought there was something very sad and yet hopeful about it.

The queen was somewhat taken aback but quickly recovered, "Well, of course my king! Whatever you want." Here she turned to Mick, suddenly all business. "What are your talents and skills? Are you trained in the skills of war?"

Mick squared his shoulders and looked the queen in the eyes, "I have some basic skills in sword play; I ride well, but my real talent is that I am a musician – a player of the flutes.

"A musician!" there was an edge of scorn to her sweet voice. "Those are more numerous than fleas on a dog around here! But… with some training, we will make a soldier of you yet. Honest men are hard to find."

"Please, Your Majesty, you should ask him to play." It was the stable boy still standing quietly holding the red horse's lead.

Queen Vanora turned sharply to him about to give a sharp reply, but then reconsidered. "Yes, let's hear you play something!...Something for a king's birthday perhaps."

"As you wish, Your Majesty." Mick pulled out his flute pouch from his nearby saddlebag and selected a small silver flute. *"High King, let me play for your joy."* Once again, Mick closed his eyes, shutting out the fact that he was playing for Livia's King and Queen and focused on how to express joy to his true king, the High King of heaven.

The silvery notes began to dance from the flute as the notes seemed to laugh and skip their way into the hearts of the listeners. Every toe began tapping and smiles began to appear on all faces within earshot. The king, who had continued to stroke Raneous' white head, began to smile and then slowly his countenance brightened. As Mick continued to play, King Jerald finally threw back his head and let out a great laugh. It was like some dark cloud lifted from his soul and he began to clap along with the music. "Oh, wonderful! Wonderful! You have done my heart a great good!" King Jerald looked from Raneous to Mick. "What a wonderful birthday present! My dear queen, he must play for me often. It is medicine to my soul."

"Why...yes of course, but we don't want to tire you out too much before tonight's party." The queen seemed a little uncomfortable with this sudden turn in the king's state of mind and seemed uncertain of what to make of it.

Mick bowed, "I would be most honored King Jerald, to play for you whenever you wish if it will do you any good."

"Then it's settled." Queen Vanora drew herself up to her full height. "Mitchell of Greensboro, you are now a member of the King's Guard with the extra duty of King's Minister of Music. Your horse will become the king's personal mount as he has requested. Your stable boy will continue to serve with you. You will report to the Captain of the Guard after the birthday celebrations have ended tomorrow." Queen Vanora then turned to her husband, "Come my dear, we must hurry back to continue our preparations for your birthday. The horse must stay here for now." With that she firmly took the king's reluctant hand off the stallion and hurried him from the stables.

The group stood at attention until the stable doors closed and they were alone except for the stable boy and the red horse. Everyone let out a sigh of relief.

The red stallion continued to stand stock still staring at the ground. He was even ignoring Raneous.

"Well, I guess I'll get this fellow some fresh hay and some oats. Maybe then his mood will improve." the stable boy said as he observed the red horse's demeanor. "And I think I'll move him down farther to be away from that white horse of yours. By the way, I'm Ben"

"Well Ben, thanks for helping us out earlier." Mick smiled at the boy.

"Oh sure! Hey, I'll be back. I got to get some oats. Do you think he misses the gypsy woman?"

Right then the red horse snorted rudely. Mick raised his eyebrows in surprise. "He doesn't seem to be in mourning; he seems to be mad or upset."

"Well, I'll do my best by him, sir. I really will. He'll come around." Ben closed the stall and headed for the door.

*

They were alone. Brian turned to Raneous. "Well, for good or bad you are now the king's personal mount. What have we gotten ourselves into? I can't stay here a year! My parents need me at the farm! And what was that between you and that other horse?... Wait!" Brian looked hard at Raneous (who was not speaking). " Is that the red horse from the Darklands?"

Raneous nodded and his nostrils flared. Mick was puzzled. "What do you mean? A horse from the Darklands? Is he evil? I didn't know demons had horses."

"They don't, but this horse used to be a part of the Heavenly Host like Raneous. Only something really bad happened to him and he quit serving the High King. He was caged like I was, when I was a prisoner in the Darklands." Brian swallowed hard as he remembered that dark and torturous place. He dropped his voice to a whisper, "He didn't leave with us, I remember, so I'm not sure how he came to be here. But you can bet he is probably a spy for the enemy so we need to be really careful what we say around him, because he is like Raneous in that he is intelligent like us."

"Well, doesn't that beat all. The world gets stranger and stranger." Mick scratched his head in wonder . "No wonder he's so big!"

"Leave it to Raneous, Mick. He will find out what he's up to. If I remember right, he was not completely controlled by the dark side, or at least he seemed to think he wasn't."

"Well, we can't wait because everything is happening tonight and we need to know where he stands." Mick looked suspiciously at the red stallion.

"Hey there, I'm back!" It was Ben with the oats. I brought your horse some oats too, since you don't know where the supplies are kept yet." Ben handed Brian a bucket full of oats.

Brian breathed in the sweet, nutty aroma, "Mmmmm! I could almost eat it raw!"

At this, Raneous gave a tug on the oats bucket with his teeth. "Oh, okay! I promise you will get it all!" Brian laughed dumping the oats into Raneous' feed trough.

Ben laughed, "That horse has a great personality! Well, gotta go. There's a huge party tonight in case you didn't remember. If you didn't get an invitation to anything, the town square will be full of music and festivities. The pie throwing contest is my favorite! See you !" The stable doors slammed shut once again.

As soon as he was gone, Raneous said softly, "Open the stall gate, Brian. I'll go visit Rune and see what I can find."

"Rune! So 'Horse' actually has a name!" Mick said, still amazed at this whole development.

The clop, clop of Raneous' hooves on the brick floor echoed as he made his way to Rune's stall.

The red horse glared at Raneous. "So, we meet again! How are you enjoying your earthbound existence, White One?"

Raneous looked at the war horse with pity, but said, "I'm not earthbound, Rune, as you are. But before I tell you my story, I want to know why you are here. Are you a spy?"

Rune looked a little surprised but snorted in disgust. "Remember, I work for no one! I'm not a spy for anyone."

"Then why are you here with us?" Raneous asked still unconvinced.

Rune sighed, "Well, if you must know, I will tell you but it's a boring story.

"I'm all ears." Raneous replied

"As you know I chose to stay in the Darklands when you made your grand exit out of there with all those people. And there I stayed until I was brought to a demon named Murmel. He proceeded to tell me that a gypsy woman needed a horse to pull her cart. I laughed and asked if he was serious and when did demons start providing transportation to needy gypsies? I got a flick from his whip for that remark, but nothing more -he wouldn't dare!

Apparently, the woman uses a crystal ball, and one afternoon Murmel paid her a visit by appearing to her. He told her he needed her to direct some travelers to the Ancient Path. She's a sharp one and asked what was in it for her. Murmel offered the use of me in exchange for getting those travelers (which turned out to be you) redirected to this path and for some ongoing service as needed. As long as she has me, Murmel uses her for whatever his need is. But yesterday, she came to the city with her cart hoping to sell a lot of trinkets for this birthday party and some soldiers, seeing that I was a stallion, forced her to go to the Captain of the Guard. She was furious and threatened all kinds of evil against him. Of course, he had her carried off and put in stocks and took me. And of course, I know she won't stay there long. I noticed that the queen has a serpent ring that matches the one the gypsy woman is always playing with. You can believe she is in the queen's service in some way.

So that is my story. I am here by chance and I continue to stay neutral in the scheme of things. I serve no one." Rune lowered his head to munch on the fresh oats Ben had left him.

Raneous looked steadily at the red stallion and felt he was telling the truth - at least as he knew it. For the first time, Raneous realized where Rune's thinking was wrong. "You say you are neutral. You say you serve no one, but you do. There is no neutral ground. In being a pawn for Murmel, you caused servants of the High King suffering and loss. If not for the power of the High King, we would have been destroyed. That gypsy would not have been able to lead us off track if you were not pulling her cart. Therefore, you are working for Murmel, who works for the Great Dragon. He lets you think you have power, but the reality is that you are earthbound and you are their prisoner until you choose to serve the High King again. And…nothing happens by chance."

Anger flared in Rune's dark eyes, but the truth of it was not lost on him. But he was proud and had spent many centuries shutting others out.

Trust and humility does not come easily to a hard heart. "So, you say you are not earthbound. Then why are you still here?" Rune's lip curled.

"I truly am here by choice, Rune. I made it back to the Brightlands. Once I reconnected with the High King's spirit, and his love, the door to the heavens was opened to me and I was able to return. I was restored to my complete self. The High King gave me a choice, Rune, to come back and live here and serve him this way. My wings are there when I need them, the power of the High King flows in me, and he is my guide and my compass." Raneous looked beseechingly at Rune, "He will do the same for you, Rune. He remembers you and aches for you."

Something flickered in the red horse's eyes. Was it hope? But it quickly disappeared. The anger, however, was gone as he said dully, "I cannot, but know this. I will not knowingly move against you or your mission here." A fire lit in Rune's eyes, "And I will NOT serve this wretched king and his guard!"

Raneous sighed but knew there was no point in pushing it further. Still, he felt he had made a point and that it had hit its mark. He returned to Mick and Brian who were anxiously waiting. "He will do us no harm intentionally." This was all he said. "Now we wait."

17- QUEEN VANORA

After Rhyse took his leave, Roslyn felt very alone as she continued in to the grand entrance of the castle. It was up to her to set their plan in action. She was the one assigned to get the serpent ring from the queen to Rhyse. She suddenly felt very small and young. Roslyn took a quivering breath and reminded herself that she wasn't alone. Auntie Anna had pulled her aside early that morning and told her she would have some inside help with her task...a handmaiden named Tess and someone else whom she could not name for security's sake.

"And," she reminded herself, *"The High King is with me!"*

Roslyn stuck out her small chin and squared her shoulders. *"It's just like before a big performance. I just have to stay calm and focused on what my part is."*

The performance party was now separating into their various groups of actors, dancers, and acrobats and moving off in different directions according to their leader's instructions. Roslyn stuck with her mother, Ms. Tabitha, as she was going to be coordinating the dancers. They wound up a long circular stairway and then down a long spacious hall decorated in rich tapestries, artistic sculptures, and beautiful vases and paintings. Closed doors that led into rich living quarters for the royal family lined this long hallway. Ms. Tabitha stopped at one large oak door and produced a big brass key from her pocket.

"Here we are, my dears! Get yourselves put together and begin warming up as soon as you are able." Ms. Tabitha said, as she opened the door into what turned out to be a beautiful large dressing room with plenty of mirrors and dressing tables for everyone.

Ms. Tabitha turned to her daughter, "Roslyn, honey, it's so wonderful to see you, though I would rather you be away from all the craziness in this city! Anna told me she needed you here. Just put yourself to good use and help out wherever it's needed." Ms. Tabitha gave Roslyn a motherly kiss on the cheek and quickly moved on to her next task.

Roslyn spent the next couple of hours doing just that. The time flew by as Roslyn assisted in sewing up a torn bodice, helped with hair arrangements and makeup, and went over choreography with a flustered dancer.

"The opening ceremony will begin in fifteen minutes!" Ms. Tabitha announced. "While the king and queen are addressing the people on the balcony, we are to get to our places in the banquet hall. There we will have an opportunity to run through our program while everyone is outside. We must be quick because once the parade is over, we need to be out of sight…"

"KNOCK! KNOCK!"

Ms. Tabitha turned to see a young woman poke her head inside the door with a hesitant smile.

"So sorry to interrupt, but we have a small emergency and I was told you might be of help." The young lady came in and curtsied briefly to Ms. Tabitha. " My name is Tess and one of the queen's handmaidens has fallen ill and cannot attend the queen. We absolutely need the help as the queen will be changing clothes several times during the celebration. Do you have anyone to spare who would be of service?"

Recognizing Tess's name, Roslyn immediately stepped forward before her mother could answer. "I am available and would be honored to help in any way." She curtsied to the handmaiden." I am Roslyn."

Ms. Tabitha, with a relieved look, said, "Of course! Roslyn is not performing tonight so that is perfect."

Tess looked Roslyn up and down considering her simple dress, nodded and smiled. "Thank you so much! We must hurry and get you changed into something more festive, since you will be in the presence of Queen Vanora" As they made their way down the hall towards the queen's handmaidens' chambers, Tess said, "We don't get to see much of the festivities but there is a lot of wonderful food!"

Roslyn wondered if she should say anything to Tess concerning her mission, but given the direction of the conversation, she decided that Tess didn't want anything said. The butterflies began to lift off in Roslyn's stomach. "I'm not sure I could eat anything anyway." She confessed.

Tess made short order of getting a very pretty, rose colored gown for Roslyn and attending to her hair. "You look like you've been attending everyone but yourself!" she commented brightly. Roslyn laughed as, in fact, that was the case.

"We don't have time for curls so I will do some nice braided patterns." Tess said even as her fingers began flying through Roslyn's hair making beautiful, even plaits. "Now let me see!" Tess looked Roslyn over with a critical eye. "Yes! Beautiful! And the girl makes the hair and dress even more so!" she said with a smile.

Roslyn blushed under this complement, but as she gazed at herself in the mirror, she had to admit the gown and hair suited her well. "You are very talented."

Tess laughed, "It's my job to make the women around here look amazing! Come! We must be ready when the queen arrives back from the opening ceremonies. The queen must always look bright and fresh. She will want to change before dinner into something more comfortable and loose and she may change again for the firework display. The banquet will have entertainment right afterwards, so it will last a good two hours. ." Tess looked pointedly at Roslyn.

It slowly dawned on Roslyn that Tess was giving her the schedule. So, she would have a two hour window to get the ring to Rhyse and hopefully get it back again before Queen Vanora came back for her final change of wardrobe.

A blonde handmaiden with pretty blue eyes popped her head in. "Tess! There you are! Queen Vanora will be returning shortly. We must get to her dressing room. The girl eyed Roslyn curiously. "I see you found some help. That's a relief!" The girl clicked the door shut and was gone.

Tess turned and looked seriously at Roslyn and said quietly, "You are to follow my instructions carefully and imitate my manners when in the presence of the queen."

Roslyn nodded solemnly and took a deep breath. "Got it."

Tess and Roslyn quickly made their way down the stone hallway of the castle to a large oak door beautifully carved with a woodland scene of deer and foxes.

"The queen's chambers." Tess said and pushed the heavy door open.

Roslyn blinked in wonder at the wealth and riches that surrounded her. The room smelled of perfume and talc powder. In the middle of the room was a huge three-way mirror and on either side were open doors to closets where Roslyn could see rows of fine dresses hanging on hooks, and rows of shoes on shelves. A plush, red rug lay on the stone floor and a fire blazed in a great stone fireplace to her left. A large wing-backed armchair and foot stool were placed conveniently close. To the right of the mirror, a delicate vanity of cherry and marble was covered with perfume bottles, lotions and powders. Three other handmaidens were bustling around the room setting things in order. All stopped as they heard the clicking sound of heels on the stone floor in the hallway.

"She's here! Places everyone!" Tess whispered loudly as she turned and faced the door. The door opened and a tall, elegant woman dressed in a long, silver satin dress appeared. Behind her came Queen Vanora. They were talking easily with each other about what to do with the queen's hair for the banquet.

The handmaidens dropped into a curtsy at the sight of the queen, who nodded briefly to them as she entered. Tess whispered to Roslyn, "That is the queen's lady- in-waiting and she is in charge."

The lady- in-waiting led the queen to stand before the mirror and nodded to the girls who promptly began to unbutton the many rows of buttons down the queen's back and down her wrists. The dress she had on for the opening ceremony was a deep, red velvet with gold trimmings and lined with what looked like a hundred gold buttons to Roslyn's untrained eye.

"Tess, please go select shoe options for a sky blue satin and pearl gown." The lady- in- waiting, whose name was Maria, directed.

Roslyn followed Tess into the royal closet and Tess began to load her up with shoes until she could barely see over the top. "Her Majesty loves shoes!" Tess smiled.

When they returned to the dressing area, the queen was down to her shift and a handmaiden was applying a cool cloth to her neck and shoulders. Maria was showing her a stunning satin gown in the palest of blues trimmed in tiny pearls and flowers.

Maria was saying, "This is the perfect dress for you, Your Majesty! You have shown your royal self to the crowds and now it is time to show your softer side.

Queen Vanora eyed the dress doubtfully. "I think it's too soft, Maria. I need something with more punch and drama."

Maria pursed her lips thoughtfully before answering, "Your Majesty, there is some talk being whispered in the courts that you are trying to control the king. This is the king's birthday, and it would be wise to be seen at the banquet with him in the image of the beautiful, feminine companion that you are, and not the strong, ambitious queen that some say you are."

The queen was surprisingly not offended at this remark but only nodded, "Yes, as always, you are right. You, Maria, have perfect fashion sense. Let them see the soft, sweet, devoted Vanora tending to her beloved husband on his birthday."

Roslyn had to admit that the pale blue satin and pearl gown was stunning on the raven haired queen and certainly had the desired effect. But Maria was just getting warmed up to her task. She began expertly applying hot, iron curling tongs to the queen's hair producing perfect ringlets. The shoes were next and after much deliberation, it was agreed that the silver satin heels studded with pearls were the perfect fit.

"Now for your jewelry, Your Majesty," Maria announced."We haven't much time left so we must be quick. Of course, being fashionably late is always a wonderful entrance and gives everyone a chance to see your amazing beauty from head to toe." She turned to the waiting handmaidens. "Bring the jewelry chests forward and let's see what we have."

A young lady curtsied, presenting a small silver chest. "I believe this will be perfect!" she commented.

And so it was. For when the small chest was opened, Maria drew out a long string of pearls intermixed with blue sapphires and diamonds. Earrings, a bracelet and a ring were also included.

Queen Vanora gazed at them. "Yes, I haven't seen those in awhile. They belonged to the King's first wife. They are exquisite, Maria! I must wear them!" She quickly placed the pearl and sapphire ring on her middle finger – right next to the serpent ring. The necklace was draped over the front of her gown in multiple strands adding just the right amount of sparkle to the already gorgeous dress.

All paused and looked at the finished product as the queen turned slowly around in front of the mirror.

Maria bit her lip in thought as she studied the effect, "Perfect! Except for one thing. That serpent ring is like a jarring note in the middle of a perfect melody! Your Majesty, it must go!"

Vanora's left hand flew protectively over the precious ring, her eyes immediately defensive and wary. Maria was not moved but waited with quiet confidence. Finally, the queen sighed reluctantly.

"I again bow to your good sense, Maria. Snakes, pearls and sweetness do not mix." Vanora reluctantly removed the ruby eyed ring and placed it in Maria's waiting hand. Maria promptly turned to Tess who had the ring chest ready and waiting. Carefully the ring was placed in the chest and locked in full view of the queen's watchful eyes. Maria handed Tess the key.

Tess then turned to Roslyn, whose heart was beating rapidly, and directed, "Place this chest in the back of the closet on the top shelf." As she handed Roslyn the chest, Roslyn felt the cold metal of the key pressed into her palm. Roslyn quickly turned to do as she was bidden knowing that the impossible had just been accomplished. She had the ring! As she entered the deep closet, she was aware that she was completely out of sight from everyone. Quickly, before she could think too much about what she was about to do, she unlocked the small chest with a soft click. The serpent ring glinted at her as she raised it from its resting place. Quietly she reached under her skirts and pulled out a small draw- string pouch she had pinned to her under slip that morning. The dress she wore had a wide sash belt around the waist into which she now securely tucked the pouch. It had to be easily gotten to when needed. Roslyn quietly returned to her place next to Tess just in time to drop a curtsy to the queen as she left for the banquet.

Unknown to Roslyn, her actions did not go unnoticed. A black, medium sized rat with yellow eyes peeked its head out from behind a blue velvet hat in the royal closet. It glared at Roslyn's back as she exited and quickly scurried down a drain pipe in the stone floor. *"She has the ring! Murmel must be alerted!"*

18- RHYSE'S TEST

"Okay, then. Here we are." Rhyse looked around and he seemed to be alone. He was standing at the foot of a steep spiral staircase that wound up a castle turret. He adjusted the heavy rope that he had coiled over his left shoulder. With the same hand he also carried three good sized arrows that had rings attached to their tails. He had just come from his Papa's private store room within the castle. In his right hand he still had his balance pole. Rhyse carefully made his way up the narrow stairway and was relieved when he met no one coming down. When he reached the top and peered out the long, narrow tower window, he was looking out over the royal stables. "Bull's eye!" To Rhyse's immense relief he also saw a small stash of weapons to the side – one of which was a cross bow. "Double bull's eye!"

Looking across to a small loft window in the stable roof, he gave a sharp, short whistle. Immediately, Brian stuck his head out and waved briefly.

Rhyse took a deep breath. He had seen his father do this but had never attempted it himself. Carefully he attached the hook that was at the end of the rope to the ring on one of the arrows, and fitted the arrow into the crossbow. Resting the crossbow on the window ledge, he motioned to Brian to get out of the way. The goal was to shoot the arrow through the window of the stable where Brian could then attach the rope to a ring that had been previously attached there years before.

Rhyse let his breath out slow and pulled the trigger. "THUD!" The arrow sank into the wooden shutter just right of the stable's window.

"BLAST!" Rhyse muttered. But Brian waved to him as he was able to reach the embedded arrow. With a little effort and a grunt, he pulled it out and pulled the rope tight. Rhyse pointed to the heavy ring attached to the stable wall just under the loft window. Brian deftly clipped the rope in place even as Rhyse did the same on his end. The rope sprang tight and now all he needed was Roslyn to give him the package.

Of course, it would be awhile so he settled down on the floor of the watch tower, with his head leaned up against the wall, to wait. Eventually he dozed off.

Rhyse awoke with a start. By the shadows on the wall he instantly knew that it was later. The next moment, he realized why he had awakened.

A large, six foot snake was coiling rapidly around his legs and trying to squeeze them together as he lay sprawled on the floor!

"HEY!!" Rhyse yelled and quick as a flash was able to free one leg. The snake hissed angrily, trying to throw another loop around the free leg. Rhyse lunged to the left and pulled with all his might. He was able to drag himself within reach of the stored weapons. He reached hard with his right hand and kicking with his free leg, he was able to knock a sword out of its stand. It clattered to the floor with a metallic ring. Rhyse grasped the hilt with both hands and swung it down as hard he could on the scaly coils stretched between his two legs. He succeeded in cutting a large gash deep into the snake's body.

The python began to writhe in agony as it released Rhyse. It tried to make its escape out of the tower window, bleeding red down the stone wall. But the boy was quick and before it could heave itself out of the window; he brought the sword down right behind its head, chopping it off completely. The body writhed and twitched in death as the red light in its eyes faded. Rhyse shuttered in disgust and shivered a little as the red blood pooled on the stone floor and turned black.

"Nasty things, these snakes!" Rhyse leaned over with his hands on his knees to catch his breath. From the noises outside, he decided the opening ceremony must be over. He needed to be on the lookout for his sister.

*

With the ring securely in her sash, Roslyn excused herself from the queen's handmaidens with the comment of checking back in with her mother. Once in the hallway, she turned left instead and made her way to the backside of the castle. She knew the tower where she was to meet her brother, as her father had tight roped across it two years ago with a basket of candy balanced on his head. Her father, once on the other side, had then thrown candy down to the delighted children and adults below. Roslyn smiled at the memory in spite of her nervousness.

"There!" a small oak door was set deep in the side of the castle wall. Roslyn looked casually around and then gave the iron ring a tug. The door opened to reveal a small and narrow arched passage that led to another oak door. "This should be it." She slowly pulled open the door. "Eeeeew!!! What is that smell?" she gasped as she saw Rhyse sitting on the tower's window ledge. The door led right to the top of the tower as she remembered.

Rhyse grinned, "I killed my first dragon!"

Roslyn looked at the nasty remains of the python. "It smells like its already rotting or something."

Rhyse nodded, "They are definitely not normal. Do you have the ring?"

Rosyln triumphantly produced the draw- string pouch. "It was so amazing, Rhyse! I couldn't believe it worked! But, we have about two hours before we need to get it back."

"Then I need to get going, because I can't run over this rope, you know. It's all set and ready." Rhyse tucked the pouch into his vest pocket and buttoned it closed. He took a deep breath and stepped up onto the window ledge with his balance pole.

"You don't have any safety wires or nets, Rhyse. Mom would die if she saw you!"

"Don't tell me things like that right now, sis! Especially don't mention dying!"

"Sorry!...You will do great!" Roslyn corrected while silently praying that the High King would protect her brother. Fearing she would be missed by the other handmaidens if she was gone too long, she said goodbye, and returned back through the passageway.

Rhyse stood on the window ledge of the tower. It was not the tallest in the castle –about three stories- but tall enough that if he fell and hit the cobblestone street below, it would not be pretty. Carefully, he stepped out onto the rope with his slippered feet. There was little wind and the rope was taut. This should not be hard. Slowly, with his balance pole swaying slightly, he stepped one foot over the other. Brian, on the other side chewed his thumbnail nervously as he watched. This back part of the castle yard seemed deserted as everyone was either at the town square or in the castle tending to the birthday party.

"There! I'm half way!" Rhyse said to himself as he continued to focus on the rope in front of him. "WHOOSH!" A gust of wind came out of nowhere! Rhyse swayed but crouched lower using the balance pole to steady himself.

Brian, looking on, caught his breath. Then he noticed something else. His scalp prickled. "What was that black thing that appeared at the tower window?"

Brian squinted and shaded his eyes in an effort to see. "A rat!" To Brian's horror, the rat began chewing on the tight rope!

"Rhyse! The rope!..." was all he could get out when the unthinkable happened.

"POP!" The rope snapped!

Brian's warning was just quick enough that Rhyse's cat-like instincts kicked in as he felt the rope give way under his feet. The balance pole clattered to the cobblestones far below, but as the rope fell away, Rhyse lunged for it. Catching hold with one hand, he was able to wrap his leg around it, saving himself from certain death. Falling now with the rope, Rhyse crashed heavily into the side of the stable wall about two stories up. Brian peered anxiously over the loft window ledge and was relieved to see Rhyse's face looking up at him as he hung next to the stable wall below. Rhyse grimaced in pain as he had slammed his shoulder heavily into the unforgiving wall.

Rhyse tried to over hand it up, but the pain in his shoulder screamed at him and there was no strength in his arm. Rhyse dangled there and considered his options. He looked down. The sight below gave him a shiver. Large, black rats – at least ten, maybe more- were gathering at the bottom. Their yellow eyes glittered and they leered up at him showing their sharp teeth. Nope, he had to go up!

Brian was a step ahead of Rhyse in thought. He peered over the edge of the loft where Mick and Raneous waited down on the stable's floor. "Mick! I need you up here now!" he whispered savagely.

Mick reached the top of the ladder in short order. After quickly assessing the situation, together he and Brian hauled Rhyse up and over the loft's ledge and safely onto the loft's plank floor. They all sat for a moment breathing heavily.

Rhyse noted, "I can't go back that way. We are going to have to figure out another way to get the ring back…and Roslyn doesn't know." Rhyse winced again as he rubbed his shoulder. "Darn rats!"

"You're lucky to be alive!" Mick answered. You've done your part so you just rest here for now. You got the ring still?"

Rhyse nodded as he unbuttoned his vest pocket and produced the small pouch. "Here it is, safe and sound!"

Mick took the pouch and tucked it safely away. "They tried to stop you but they failed. We'll figure out the rest later, but now we need to get to the crypt!"

19- INTO THE CRYPT

Raneous, Mick and Brian stood in front of the door of the large crypt. They felt sure they hadn't been followed. Brian wondered if this might be because of Raneous. A rat, even a demonic one, is no match for a Brightlander stallion. All was quiet in the cemetery. The stone archway of the crypt was ancient and the ivy that covered most of it seemed almost as old.

They all looked at each other in anticipation. "Well, here we go." Mick held his ring hand up. He had placed the ring on his pinky finger before leaving the stables. Sure enough, a medium sized python snake dropped down out of the ivy to inspect his offering. Its eyes glowed red matching the ruby eyes in the serpent ring. Slowly, the heavy stone door swung silently inward revealing a musty darkness and the beginning of stone steps leading downward. The three quickly entered, their hearts beating rapidly in their chests. Raneous' hooves echoed loudly on the stone steps.

"Shhh!" Mick hushed. Quickly, Brian lit the lantern he had brought from the stable and lifted it to look around. The door behind them closed shut with an ominous click. They were in!

Ten broad steps led down to the stone floor where a large stone coffin sat. Its lid was carved with the majestic figure of an ancient Livian king.. Brian sensed that they were now underground. There were statues and carvings along the walls – the apple tree seemed to be a main theme.

"Not too scary." Brian thought to himself. *"Be brave now!"*

"Look!" Brian whispered and pointed to the back of the crypt. Where the back wall should have been, gaped an enormous round hole or tunnel instead. The stone wall had been burrowed through, and the tunnel sloped gently down into the earth. Cautiously, they made their way forward until they were standing at the yawning entrance.

Mick pointed to the smooth dirt floor, "Footprints! And lots of them!" he whispered. "Who wants to go first?"

"Actually, we can all go together." Brian pointed out. "It's a big tunnel." Even their whispers echoed off the stone walls making Brian feel as if they were announcing their arrival to anything below. "Raneous, you get in the middle." he directed. Then they began a careful descent. Brian held the lantern high with one hand and kept his other hand in Raneous' mane. The walls of the tunnel were completely smooth. It reminded him of something he'd seen before, but where? He searched his mind trying to find the image. Suddenly, he remembered. It reminded him of a hole in the ground that a bug had crawled out of - perfectly round, perfectly smooth. Giant bugs were not what Brian wanted to think about, so he pushed those thoughts away hastily with a shiver.

The tunnel continued downward sometimes curving to the right, sometimes to the left. They continued on for some time, always going down.

"Hold up!" Brian whispered, "I think there's a wall." He lifted his lantern higher, "It's a fork to both the left and right."

Raneous stepped forward and sniffed, first to the right and then to the left. "The right tunnel leads deeper into the earth. The left side...." He pricked his ears and listened intently. "I hear something. Its sounds like a humming. Let's go left." He did not mention that out of the depths of the right tunnel he sensed something evil lurking deep within.

The three went left and within a few feet the humans could hear the noise too. Humming or maybe chanting was a better word, for now it seemed there were words being spoken in a chant-like rhythm. Cautiously, they all moved forward and they began to see a soft glow of light ahead. Everyone's hearts were beating rapidly now. What could this be? The tunnel opened up into an enormous room. The ceiling was so tall the light could not reach it. Then they saw the source of the sound. A lone, robed and hooded person was chanting and walking among round objects on the cavern floor. Occasionally, he would stop and carefully turn one. Now the travelers saw that these round objects covered the entire floor of the cavern. Hundreds of them lay in ordered rows. The robed person had his back to the three visitors as he was walking and chanting in an unknown language.

In a moment of revelation, all three understood. Mick gasped, "Eggs!"

The chanting abruptly stopped and the robed figure swiftly turned at the sound. Seeing the three, he started towards the strangers, "What is the meaning of this? Who are you? No one is to disturb this sanctuary!"

Mick hesitated. There was something familiar in the man's voice — for it was a man. "Sam? Sam, is that you?"

The face of the man was shaded by the hood but Brian could see the glint of his eyes in the lantern light as they cut sharply to look at Mick. The hooded man gasped in surprise, "Why, brother! Is that you? Have you come to join our great plan? I will make you great, for I have ascended to greatness in the realm! I, who used to only speak on behalf of the king, now I speak forth words that will bring down kingdoms and raise new ones up!"

Sam dramatically threw back his hood. Mick's joy at finding his brother quickly turned to shock when he saw the look of arrogant ambition on his brother's face. His brother had changed! Sam's thick blonde hair had been shaved off and his eyes had a slightly glazed look to them, but the arrogance and pride were unmistakable in his eyes and the curve of his mouth.

"Sam!.. Samuel! What have you gotten yourself into?" Mick stepped forward and grasped his brother's shoulders firmly. "I have been searching for you! The High King has sent me and my friends here to help you." Still in shock, Mick looked at this new Sam. " Now, my question is, do you want to be helped?"

"Release me, Mick! I have found where my gifts are appreciated. Here, I speak forth ideas and visions and they become these beautiful eggs, full of power. Once they are ready to hatch, they are moved to another chamber where they are fed and nurtured until they are strong enough to live on their own. My words, my visions are then sent forth into the kingdom to influence people's minds and thoughts. This is true power, my brother! I will teach you!"

It was Brian who spoke up then, "What are "THEY". It sounds like your ideas become something alive."

Sam ignored the question and stepped quickly back out of Mick's grasp. "Don't you see? The old way of doing things is…well…old!" Sam's eyes glinted. "Our queen is taking us into a new form of government, but the old one must fall. When we are finished, all the regions of the Shadowlands will be united. There will be no more division. It will be one, big unified kingdom!" Sam's eyes got that far away look as he envisioned this grand future and his great role in it.

Mick snorted in disgust, "And ruled by whom? Queen Vanora and all her demonic snakes and rats?"

"Of course not, idiot brother!" Sam snarled back. "She is a servant just as I am. There will be one central council and…"

"WHAT?! And who's leading the council, Sam?" Mick's voice rose in anger.

"Oh, my dear brother I know you don't understand, but there are great powers at work here; powers that are far wiser than we are." Sam nodded knowingly.

Mick's eyes welled up with tears, "Sam! Don't you see? The Great Dragon and his demons are using your gifts for their purposes! You and I were both born with strong gifts that are powerful. You, Sam, are a prophet by gifting; a born prophet, called to serve your Creator the High King, and I am called to sing his praises. Both are powerful and both can be badly twisted and cause great damage if misused. Mick reached for his brother again, "Come away from here, Sam, and find your TRUE calling! You are meant to be giving messages of hope, messages for strategy, messages that inspire courage! You are NOT meant to be hiding down here in a dark stink hole breathing worthless lies!" Mick, seeing that his words were falling on deaf ears, turned and angrily began crushing eggs under his feet.

"NOOOOO!!!! My precious eggs! My precious ones!!" Sam began to desperately pick up and gather into his robes as many eggs as possible in an effort to save them.

With a high whinny, Raneous joined Mick and began stomping. "CRUNCH, CRUNCH, CRUNCH!!" Brian hesitated only for a second and then he too began crushing eggs. Under Brian's feet the eggs broke easily. When he picked his foot off the first one, he saw a tiny undeveloped snake. Writhing around in the dust, it turned black and died.

Then the ground beneath their feet began to tremble and shake, and a low rumble could be heard from the passage behind them. Something was moving against the earthen walls in the tunnel below them – something very large!!

20- BREATH OF FIRE

In one motion, Brian, Mick and Raneous turned back to the tunnel's mouth to face this new terror. Raneous stomped the ground with his hoof. A light burned in his eyes and Brian recognized the battle fury coming upon him.

"On my back Brian! We will face this thing together! FOR THE HIGH KING AND TO HIS GLORY!!"

Brian leapt onto the stallion's back and suddenly, he felt the weight of his sword and holster sling against his right hip. The horse's giant wings beat the air around him. Brian looked down at Mick and saw that he too was arrayed for battle; dressed in white and a sword drawn. Mick was looking somewhat astonished at his change, but nodded encouragingly to Brian. The High King's power to fight was upon them all, but as Brian turned back to look at the tunnel entrance, his blood ran cold in spite of the High King's divine weapons.

The head of an enormous red python snake was emerging from the right tunnel! Its head looked to measure about three feet across. Brian swallowed hard and did not want to think what that meant for the rest of its body. This was his worst nightmare come true! "Hold it together, Brian!" he muttered under his breath. The head and scaly body kept coming up, up, and up until it towered over them; its wicked red eyes were angry and murderous as it flicked its black forked tongue at the unwelcome intruders.

"Who has DARED to desecrate this sanctuary?!" It hissed. But it already knew for it recognized the power of the High King in front of it. The snake stared at the winged horse in front of it and hissed. "You are no match for me! I have penetrated into the minds and hearts of this city and I AM STRONG!! With this last statement it opened its mouth wide. Brian, Raneous and Mick were staring into rows of sharp teeth while wisps of blue smoke spewed from the snake's nostrils.

Brian, even at this moment found himself thinking, "*So, when did pythons ever have big teeth…and breath fire?!*"

"*When they are bred in the Darklands.*" the unexpected answer came into his mind.

Raneous shook his mighty head and spoke boldly as he reared up ready to charge, "Serpent! You and your forces are defeated because NO enemy that comes against the High King will succeed!"

The snake opened its wide red mouth. Brian pointed his sword upward but felt in his heart he was getting ready to be roasted alive by fire, so in dread, he closed his eyes. "*Save us High King!*" he whispered.

There was a flash of fire and heat! Brian knew this was his end, but instantly, a blinding white light blazed even through his closed eyes. Fearfully, he looked and saw an amazing and beautiful sight! A mighty warrior angel was standing between the snake and them. Great orange flames of fire were blowing fiercely out of the snake's mouth, but the angel held up a large golden shield and it was absorbing and deflecting it. The angel braced himself against the onslaught and the heat. Raneous, Mick and Brian all stopped and just watched in awe.

Then the angel turned to them with a strained smile, "Umm... Could I get a little praise here, please? Some joy?" Kiran asked – for it was the same angel that Raneous had seen standing in the pine tree on the mountain. The angel was holding fast but his teeth were clenched and his muscles knotted in the effort to hold the flame at bay. "Praise him!" he urged again. "Praise the High King! This is your fight!" Again, Kiran strained to hold his golden shield up against the strength of the blistering flames.

Mick, a worshiper at heart, was the first to understand and to act. Quickly he stepped forward with his sword lifted, "The High King reigns and his kingdom endures forever! Glory and honor to his name! No other name will be held higher than his, for he is the one true and faithful! He is the victorious one and he cannot be defeated!"

The angel's shield began to grow larger and strength poured into him . "Keep it up! I'll take the heat! You attack! Never stop praising!"

Raneous then lifted off and flew high over the snake's head in order to distract it from Mick . The serpent followed their movement with its great head trying to blast them with flames, but once again, Kiran, like a beam of light, flew to their defense and absorbed the flames in his mighty shield. Brian, holding tight to Raneous as they hovered overhead, saw their chance. With the serpent's neck fully extended, Brian shouted, "Dive Raneous! I'll go for the throat!"

Down they swooped , with Brian holding tightly to Raneous' mane, he leaned out as far left as he could. Then with all his strength, he plunged his sword deep into the neck of the serpent as they flew by. "Take that! The High King reigns!" he shouted as the sword plunged deep into the red scaly throat.

Mick, down below, took advantage of the serpent's distraction with the flying horse and with praise still on his lips, began slicing at the thick body.

"To the High King!"

"WHACK!" His blade hit the hard scales of the snake and glanced off.

Mick gripped his sword hilt firmly and took a deep breath, "Your power in me High King!" and he drove the sword point into the body, piercing the red scales. Black ooze began to spill from the wound and the smell of rotten flesh filled the room. The snake, infuriated with this new source of pain, turned to blast Mick with its flames, but Kiran was faster and once again his mighty shield protected all from becoming toast.

"I've got you!" the angel yelled.

The fire quickly died from its mouth as its throat wound began to fill with blood. Savagely, with its fire extinguished, the serpent began slashing wildly with its teeth. The huge mouth swung around seeking to catch Raneous and Brian in flight. But Raneous, glowing in the power of heaven, anticipated the snake's movements, and dove under its head, while Brian, seeing the snake's weakness, lunged forward and up with all his might to sink his sword deep into the roof of the serpent's mouth and into its brain.

"The High King has delivered us from death! He has beaten the snake!" Brian shouted as the eyes of the snake went dark and the great head crashed to the ground - dead.

Raneous and Brian came to a landing beside Mick and Kiran. Then something odd began to happen. The room began to fill with whispering voices. Ugly words with evil intent filled the room. Hundreds of different voices rose and fell, but all were cursing, complaining and cutting down everything good. Then they slowly faded away.

Kiran, stood over the giant serpent head listening. He turned to the three and said, "This beast fed and grew on all the discontentment and ugliness that has made this city so miserable in the last few years. Praise and thanksgiving to the High King is the only weapon against it and others like it." The warrior smiled, "You have done very well!" He looked around at them all. "But beware, it isn't over. This serpent is a servant to Murmel and that demon must be dealt with!"

Raneous remembered the dark storm clouds he had seen coming out of the north. "No, it isn't over. We must prepare for a bigger battle; the battle for the heart and soul of Livia."

Kiran bowed his head slightly to Raneous and disappeared.

21- SAM'S RETURN

The three warriors looked in awe at each other and at the huge dead snake lying on the cave floor. Suddenly, Mick looked around, "Where is my brother?"

Quickly they turned back to the egg sanctuary to look for Sam. Huddled in a corner, and staring with wild eyes, Sam sat terrified and shaking watching them approach.

"Come no further, I beg you! Spare my life valiant warriors! I am a ruined man! All my work has been destroyed!" He looked pathetically at the three remaining eggs tucked in his robes.

"Sam! I'm your brother, Mick! Of course I'm not going to destroy you! I came here to get you out of this mess because I love you!" Mick knelt down in front of his miserable brother. "You got mislead and deceived by lies. We all make mistakes, but thanks to the High King, there is a way out!

You can put your talents to good use for the High King and for the good of Livia! You are not the enemy, brother, and neither are we!"

Sam slumped even further down and covered his eyes with his hands but he moaned, "Such power! All this time I thought that serving the High King was for school children, women and poor people. I have been serving the wrong side! All for nothing!!" In anger he threw the three remaining eggs against the wall where they splattered and died. "Nothing!"

At this point Raneous stepped forward and said gently, "Not for nothing! Now you know where the real power lies, and you know more than anyone the lies that are being told around here. With that knowledge, you can help turn this city around by using your gift of speech."

Sam looked up in wonder at the winged stallion still radiating light in the dim cavern. But the glimmer of hope in his eyes quickly died. "The High King must hate me now. He would never take me back after what I have done against him."

Brian felt a tug on his heart and he quietly slipped off of Raneous' back. He knelt by the wretched man and took his hand, and somehow Brian didn't feel awkward at all, "I know for a fact that the High King will take you if you want to be taken back. I know because he rescued me from my own bad choices that took me prisoner into the Darklands. It's no different for you. You only have to choose him."

"You? But you fought with so much strength! How is it that you were a Darkland prisoner?" Sam searched Brian's eyes. "Ah, I see there is a long story there."

Brian smiled, "Yes, a long story that I will be glad to tell you, but all you have to do is choose the High King! He is just waiting. It's your choice!"

Sam looked doubtfully from Brian to Raneous and finally back to his own brother, Mick, who was now also kneeling in front of him. "You came searching for me?"

"Sam, without the High King's help, I could never have done this myself. So, let that be proof to you that the King wants you back!" Mick took his brothers hands and raised him to his feet. "What do you say?"

A look of relief and joy spread over Sam's face and his eyes brimmed with thankful tears. "Take me, High King! I have done terrible damage against you, but if you will have me back, I will gladly serve you from my heart!"

Bright clean light shimmered around him in the dark. The dark robes disappeared and Sam looked in astonishment at the white tunic and sword slung at his side. "Why, I'm dressed just like you now!"

"That's because you ARE one of us now!" Mick laughed through his own tears of joy. "Let me introduce my friends to you; Raneous of the Brightlands, and Brian, young servant of the High King!"

Raneous brought them back to the task still at hand. "We have limited time left and we must find a way to return the queen's ring to Roslyn quickly."

As they started back up the wormhole to the crypt, Mick quickly filled Sam in on the present plan and their problem with returning the ring before the queen missed it.

"Why, I can be of help!" Sam rubbed his hands in anticipation, "I still have keys to all the castle doors and know my way to the exact tower you are describing. Let me do this, please!"

Just then, they stepped into the ancient crypt and as they did, they were returned to their normal appearance. Sam's black robes were gone, however. In their place were new court clothes. He looked with wonder at his fresh new look. Fingering his new wool green vest, he smiled, "You know, green is my favorite color!"

"For a new start!" Raneous said with a nod of his regal head.

Mick teased, "Yeah, the green hat covers your bald head nicely!" Immediately, however, he sobered as he considered their next move. "Sam, you should make your way to the castle alone now. We will wait until you are gone before we leave the crypt and return to the stables. That way we are not seen together." Mick placed the serpent ring back in its pouch and handed it to Sam who tucked it securely into his vest pocket.

Sam smiled cheerfully at them, "Don't worry, I won't let you down. I will get it to your friend." Quickly, he opened the crypt door and left.

Brian, looked around at them and realized that they were at the end of their plans. They had all thought that once they found Sam and gotten into the crypt that somehow it would be over. But the angel, Kiran, said that it wasn't over, and there was more to come. A thrill of excitement ran through Brian's body. He was fighting for the High King! He was working alongside Raneous and angels! In his wildest dreams he would have never seen this coming. The High King had somehow managed to take a tortured, bitter and abused boy and turn him into a warrior. Tears of gratefulness welled up in Brian's eyes as he thought about how he and his whole family had been truly rescued from darkness. Now, a city needed to be rescued.

Mick was speaking now and Brian's thoughts were brought back to the task at hand. "We should return to the stables and see how the High King leads us from there."

Raneous snorted and tossed his head, "We won't have to wait long, I'm sure. That demon, Murmel, will be looking for us. We killed his favorite pet snake and shook his dark world!"

22- MESSAGE FROM THE NORTH

Anna the Prophetess paced back and forth in her cottage looking towards the city of Livia. She was waiting but she did not know for what. She had a sense of expectation. Something was happening! She could feel it in her bones and in the air around her. "Well, I might as well do the wash." She sighed and began to gather up dirty aprons and shirts. The whinny of a horse caught her ears and she looked up to see a black horse and a rider also all in black travelling swiftly up her road to her cottage.

"No laundry after all," and she dropped the pile back in its basket. "Now I will hear something!" Anna went to the door to greet the unexpected visitor.

The black horse pulled up when the rider saw Anna step out onto the porch. "Greetings! Are you Anna the Prophetess?"

"I am." Anna said with a nod. She was always slightly amused at such a grand title being given to her.

The rider, Anna noticed, was probably younger than twenty and seemed worn out from a hard ride. He did not, however, forget his manners. The young man removed his black rimmed hat, "I bring you news from the northern city of Norwin. This is a special message from the prophet Omar who lives in that region."

"Please, surely you can dismount and let me give you and your horse some water and food!" Anna protested as she saw that he was going to immediately launch into his news. She also noted that the beautiful black mare's body was lathered and she had foam around her mouth and bit from a long hard journey.

The young rider, however, would not be distracted, "This is very urgent but as soon as I deliver the message we will gladly accept your hospitality." Then he looked around the apple grove. "Are we safe here to speak openly?"

Anna smiled, 'You are free to speak openly here." She smiled amusedly, because she knew the youth could not see the angels that encircled her property. "Very safe, actually."

"Very well." The young man took a deep breath. "My name is Jonathon and I am the youngest son of Omar the Prophet of the city of Norwin. A plot has recently come to my father's knowledge and he felt he must warn you of your present danger. Norwin is Queen Vanora's native town. She was raised and mentored by none other than Norwin's Counselor Thorndike. She has secretly maintained contact with him over the last two years and we just recently intercepted one of Thorndike's messages to her. It revealed much. The plot, however, is bigger than these two. They are both in league with a secret but powerful group called the Unity Council whose plan is to overthrow all the capital cities in the North, South, East and West and to unite them under one government council. Norwin was the first to fall, but Livia is next. They are doing it without war by sending gifted influential people into a kingdom who can turn people to their ideas. Norwin also had an invasion of rats and then snakes. The infestation tore the city apart and turned people against each other and their king. Our king had been growing weaker with an unknown illness and when he turned up dead one morning last week in his bed, Counselor Thorndike quickly made himself Governor with the promises of many worthy changes to the city and region. It is believed that Vanora has been slowly poisoning your King Jerald and is most likely responsible for King Jerald's first wife's death." Jonathon drew a deep breath before continuing. "I'm sorry to be a bearer of bad news, but this plot against all the Shadowlands needs to be stopped. We don't have the answer, but we know that the High King wanted this message delivered to you." Having done his job, Jonathon wearily dismounted and began to attend to his horse.

Anna, still digesting the significance of this news, retrieved a bucket of water for Jonathon's thirsty mare while the young man began to rub her down. But her thoughts were toward her High King and she prayed with passion under her breath, *"High King, you know all things and must guide me now on what to do with this information."*

The answer came soft and clear, *"Send this message to Essie at the castle to give to those who wait in the king's stables: When my children quit tearing down their king and kingdom and choose instead to praise their High King, honor their city, and its servants that I have placed over them, then I can heal Livia of its sickness. There are times that you fight to win a battle and then there are times you need to sing songs for deliverance."*

Quickly, with directions to Jonathan to make himself at home, Anna went to her pigeon coop and selected Essie's pigeon. Taking some thin parchment paper she kept in there for this purpose, she quickly but carefully wrote all she had heard the High King say. She knew there was no time to explain Jonathan's entire story to them at this time. What they needed was the next step. Once satisfied with her work, she rolled the parchment up and put it in a small cylinder attached to the pigeon's back. Anna stroked the pigeon's head softly, "Go home and find Essie!" With that, she released the pigeon from the coop and watched it head directly towards Livia.

Jonathon was sitting on her porch waiting. His dark hair was damp with sweat and he had removed his riding boots. He had finished rubbing his horse down and had put her on a picket line so that she could crop the green tender grass. He stood in his stocking feet with his hat in his hand as she approached.

"Come, you must be exhausted. Some hot food and drink will revive you. There is a wash basin in the back corner where you can refresh yourself." Anna motioned him into the cottage. "You can sleep here tonight. My nephew, Rhyse, has been sleeping in my loft. You are welcome to use his bed since he is in Livia." Anna paused and thought for a moment, "If you have no further business, I would like to ask you for some help."

Jonathon bowed, "I am at your service. Whatever I can do to assist you."

Anna smiled, "You have been raised in the court of a king! I can tell. I need you to take me into Livia at first light tomorrow morning. I must help gather and rally the High King's people. Livia is an hour by foot but we can cut that in half on horseback. There is to be a parade tomorrow morning as part of the closing ceremony in honor of King Jerald's birthday. My sister and her husband are in charge of it and I believe we can use it in our strategies."

"I gladly accept the chance to help. And whatever knowledge I learn may be of use to my city…and to others!"

"Then we leave tomorrow at dawn." Anna smiled but wondered what the new day would bring.

23- FIRE

"TAP, TAP, TAP!" Someone was tapping on the back stable door.
Mick looked around at the three. They had been filling Rhyse in on the
fight in the crypt while he sat and massaged his battered arm in an effort to
restore strength to it. Luckily nothing was broken, it was just badly bruised.
Now at the tapping sound, Mick jumped up to open the door, but it opened
itself and the very pleasant but worried face of Essie, the castle's head cook,
peered around the door.

"Excuse me! I just received an urgent message from Anna to give
to you!" She was flustered and her plump red cheeks were moist from hard
work. " Pardon me, but I can't stay. I'm in the middle of making whipped
cream, but here's the note. She quickly handed the thin rolled parchment to
Mick and was gone before they could even thank her.

Excitedly, they all gathered around as Mick carefully unrolled the
parchment and read it softly out loud to them. For a moment they all
looked at each other in puzzlement.

Mick repeated the last line, " 'There are times when you fight to win a battle and then there are times you need to sing songs for deliverance.' What does that mean?"

It was Rhyse who brightened first. "The parade for the closing ceremonies! You just got through telling me you killed a giant snake by praising the High King. What if all of the High King's servants gathered together and took over the parade? Actually, most of the dance and acrobatic companies involved are High King followers – they are under the teaching of my parents. But there are more throughout the city."

Mick nodded and then sighed, "Yes there are many, so why has Livia fallen into this trap?" He answered his own question, "Because we don't understand the kind of power we have as High King servants. Like my brother said, people who follow the High King are not really taken seriously." Mick squared his shoulders, "Those days are done! The Darklanders had better get ready because the music is about to begin!"

Raneous nodded, "It might be enough. Others may join in as they see what is happening. There is great power in unity and praise!"

"BOOM!" "POP!" " POP!" " POP!"

"Fireworks! The grand finale of tonight's festivities!" Mick said as they all listened to the popping and the whistling overhead. I hope Sam made the connection with Roslyn."

Rhyse nodded and tried not to think about what would happen if he had not. "This also means that my parents are finished for the night and now is my time to go inform them of what needs to happen tomorrow morning! I just hope they believe me. But the instructions are from Anna the Prophetess– Mom's sister! Rhyse turned once more before leaving,

"The parade always starts at the Western Gate and ends at the castle entrance in the center of the city. Gotta go catch up with my papa! Just wait 'til I tell him about the giant snake! He's gonna love it!" The back door slammed and he was gone.

"What about those nasty rats outside?" Brian questioned but Rhyse was already gone.

"I'm guessing demonic rats don't like fireworks any more than heavenly horses do!" Raneous said with his ears laid back flat against his head. "Too loud!"

KABOOM!!! Showers of sparks and splintered wood rained down on them, and everyone ducked for cover. Brian and Mick both looked up in horror even as they tried to cover their heads. A stray rocket had actually punctured through the stable's roof before it exploded. Tongues of flame now caught hungrily onto the dry roof and to everyone's horror, the stable roof was now on fire! Fire and hay are a deadly mix and horses' screams of terror filled the air. Guards and stable boys began to yell and run towards the stable and the flames.

"The horses! The horses! Get the horses out!" The Captain of the Guard was yelling even as he ran into the stables. "Water! We need the water wagon! Quick! Everyone grab a bucket!"

In all the commotion no one noticed the four in the back of the stables. Mick yelled, "Out the back door! Quick!"

The hay in the loft had caught fire and the blistering flames began to quickly spread along the walls. Mick opened the back stables doors wide, while Brian grabbed their belongings and Raneous' lead rope. He also unlatched the stall doors of the frightened neighboring horses. The frightened beasts didn't need any encouraging to leave. With the glow of the fire lighting their way, they quickly made their way back towards the cemetery. The air was now filled with the shouts of stable hands as they opened the stalls of the terrified horses as they lunged at their stall gates. The stable was emptying fast, but a deafening horse scream stopped Raneous and the two humans in their tracks and they all turned around towards the heated inferno in horror.

A horse was trapped! Raneous started to bolt back in, but Brian grimly held his lead. "You can't Raneous! Let the people do this.

They watched and to their dismay they saw the head of a beautiful stallion rise and fall as he desperately tried to kick through the stable wall. A fiery support beam had fallen from the roof and was blocking him into his stall. Brian gasped, "Oh no! It's Rune!"

Before any of them could think or move, a small figure appeared at the front stable doors.

"I'm coming! I'm coming!" It was Ben, Rune's newly appointed keeper and he was taking his job seriously.

"No boy!" came a deeper voice. "Let the men handle this!"

But Ben had already entered the flaming structure. He had doused himself with water and covered his mouth with a handkerchief. Carrying a bucket of water, he determinedly made his way through the smoke to where the panicked stallion was trapped. With one heave, he threw the water onto the lowest part of the burning beam. Then with his foot he kicked through the charred wood. Rune, seeing his path clear, bolted through the small opening knocking the boy down so hard it knocked the breath out of him. Ben lay on the brick floor struggling to breathe.

Now something incredible happened. For the first time in
centuries, Rune thought about the well being of another creature. This boy
had just risked his life for him and now he could not deny it. It appeared
the old war horse had a soft spot in his stone cold heart after all. He could
not leave Ben behind. Fighting his own panic and fear of fire, Rune stopped
himself and bent down to pick the boy up by his belt with his teeth. It was
enough to get Ben back on his feet and together they ran from the burning
building.

Everything seemed like chaos but the mounted guard and the
stable hands worked quickly and the fire came under control. The roof was
gone but most of the walls and all of the horse stalls were saved. Most
importantly, all horses and people got out alive.

"I would guess they will put the horses in the town livery until this
can be repaired." Mick commented, but he wondered how this was going to
affect their plans for tomorrow.

"There you are!" It was Ben still soaked and covered in soot. "The
captain says that you two will stay in the mounted guard's quarters tonight,
but the horse will be stabled at the town livery. Also, believe it or not the
parade for the morning is still on! The queen has said that nothing will keep
the king from celebrating his birthday properly." Ben looked over at the big
white horse. "You know, you and that horse would be welcome in the
parade. The mounted guard ride is in it and I'm sure you could just join
right in – especially since you will be bunking with them tonight."

Mick looked at Brian meaningfully, "Yes, it would be an honor to
ride for the king." To himself he thought, *"Another perfect set up by the High
King!"* A thrill went through him as he thought of all the possibilities that
tomorrow might bring.

But Raneous caught movement on burnt rafters of the stable and yellow eyes glared down at him. Yes, what would tomorrow bring?

24- THE BATTLE FOR LIVIA

At daybreak the sleepy Livians awoke to a dark and overcast sky that seemed to match their dark mood. Huge black thunderheads were rolling over the northern mountains and bringing colder winds with the smell of rain. With the fire last night, the tension in the air, and now the bad weather, the Livians were not looking to celebrate their king- the king who seemed to be the cause of all their problems. But they had no real choice except to put on a happy face and get through the closing ceremonies.

Raneous nuzzled Brian where the exhausted boy slept on the clean hay in the stall. He had insisted on staying with Raneous. Brian groggily opened his eyes, but quickly became fully awake when all the activities from the day before rushed into his mind. Quickly he sat up and began brushing hay out of his hair and seeing to Raneous' breakfast.

"Good morning to you – although the weather is dark." Ben seemed to be the ever cheerful kind of fellow. "Mick asked me to bring you some hot oatmeal. You'll need it for a long walk in the parade."

Ben handed Brian a steaming bowl and then pushed his hands into his pockets and watched the two eat. "Well, Ole Red let me brush him down last night without a fight or a kick. I guess our fire experience gave him some trust in me."

Brian hesitated but said, "You know, I know Ole Red's real name. Before he belonged to the gypsy, Raneous and I had some history with him. His name is Rune."

"Rune! Well, knowing his birth name will be real helpful when working with a stubborn horse like him." Ben smiled. "If you're ready, I'm supposed to take you and Raneous to the guard house to meet Mick. You are all going to be in the parade!"

*

Myran, from the back of his dappled mare, looked over his troop of acrobats, dancers, musicians, and singers. They in turn were looking expectantly back at him waiting for orders. There were many more Livians joining them as well since Anna and Jonathon had been busy gathering trusted High King's servants throughout the city. Myran could see the young man from the north on his black horse towards the back of the crowd. Myran looked at the gloomy sky. The cold wind blew the many banners, ribbons and garlands around as if to laugh at their efforts. His son, Rhyse, had delivered Anna's message and had also informed him of the snake slaying. Myran knew this was big and what he was about to do might cost him dearly. Though the message had been short, Myran was a perceptive man and understood what maybe his son didn't. This could be seen as treason by Queen Vanora. But Livia was under attack from the inside and from the dark side and he was not going to sit and do nothing when directions from the High King had been given. Myran recalled part of the message: "*When my children quit tearing down their king and kingdom and choose instead to praise their High King...*" There was more but basically the promise was that Livia's ugliness could be healed. When he saw the large white stallion and his two companions join his group, he made up his mind. He would do everything in his power to carry out the High King's directions!

"Listen all! Today we will be celebrating the High King and his power over darkness! Today we will dance and sing like the life of our city depends on it. Many of you were contacted last night to join this parade. Thank you for your quick response. We are singing for the deliverance of Livia from the evil that is trying to strangle her! My wife, Ms. Tabitha, has the list of songs for you." Myran caught Mick's eye and motioned him forward.

Mick, looking handsome in his black feathered hat and riding Raneous, stepped forward motioning Brian to come with him."Yes, sir?" Mick responded.

Myran smiled appreciatively at the beautiful horse. "My son has informed me that we have a visitor from the Brightlands of heaven. Myran looked back at Mick, "I am asking that you lead this parade and I will follow as a banner bearer on my mare."

Mick paused to consider but said, "Sir, I ask that I march on foot with the musicians. That is where my talent lies." Mick looked down at

Brian who now stood beside Raneous' head. "This young man here, Brian, is the rightful rider for this horse. They're a team."

Myran looked thoughtfully at Brian, a boy about his son's age he guessed. He saw the steady way Brian returned his gaze and sensed the bond between the horse and the boy. Myran nodded, "If that is what you see as best. We need everyone doing what they do best!"

Before Brian knew quite what was happening, he found himself astride Raneous at the front of the parade. He glanced back at the crowd behind him and saw Roslyn and Rhyse both wave at him, but it was Roslyn's wave that made his heart leap. It did not cure his uncertainty, however. "Mr. Myran, I don't really know the way."

"I will be riding at your shoulder flying the High King's banner. I will direct you as needed. And actually, I'm not sure what is going to happen once we get started, so stay alert! The mounted guard will go first in solumn formation. Once they are far out in front we will start our own program!" Myran looked up at the dark brooding sky again and said with bold determination, "We will start with a song of celebration!"

A lively bugle call interrupted any further thoughts. Myran shouted, "Places everyone! The Royal Mounted Guard is ready. The parade begins!"

In a short minute, all were in their places waiting for the march to begin. The sound of the mounted soldiers on their horses, the jingle of their harnesses, the clop of the many hooves, was solemn yet exciting. They all watched with admiration as the guard rode forth to the beat of the marching drummers, flags flying high in the wind. In spite of the weather, people lined up on both sides of the street to watch the magnificent war horses march by. Myran waited until the last horseman rounded the bend in the street. He raised his arm, "FORWARD! And let the praise begin!"

The pipes, the drums, the stringed instruments, and tambourines accompanied by hundreds of voices bursting into song sending fearsome vibrations of praise into the darkness around them. The sound went into the sewers and the hidden places. Within minutes rats and snakes began to pour out of the drains and holes trying to get away from this glorious praise.

Sing and rejoice O kingdom of Livia!
Sing and rejoice! The King reigns on High!
Sing and rejoice! O kingdom of Livia!
Sing and rejoice! Your deliverance has come!

As Raneous surged forward, the dancers, with streamers in hand, spread out twirling and dancing in pure joy to the great astonishment of the watching Livians. Roslyn, with a tambourine ringing clearly in the air, felt the rush of the High King's joy as she twirled and danced in the face of darkness. Rhyse, along with his fellow acrobats, did back hand springs, cartwheels and whatever came into their heads to do as they moved forward down the street in celebration of the High King. Rhyse was amazed as new strength poured into his bruised arm – the pain completely vanished!

Over and over they sang and danced this simple but powerful song through the dark and dreary streets of troubled Livia. Slowly, people began to join in with the song and some even joined the procession clapping and singing with all their might. The added voices added volume until the city was ringing with the shouts and songs of the Livian people singing praise to their High King.

Raneous and Brian, still in the lead with Myran, were nearing the center market square where the front castle gates stood. Brian looked up and could see King Jerald and Queen Vanora standing on their balcony looking on. The king was clapping with his thin hands and smiling with delight, but the queen's face was red with anger. The Captain of the Guard and his mounted men stood in formation in front of the gates, but they made no move to interfere.

Suddenly, the storm clouds brooding over the city began to boil and roll and a swirling wind began to blow. A horrible screech was heard overhead and everyone looked up in surprise and wonder. Out of the clouds, flying on bat wings, was a creature that looked part lizard but with the head of a snake.

Everyone froze in their tracks as they watched this demon descend and land on the tallest tower of the castle.

"I AM MURMEL! AND THIS CITY BELONGS TO ME!" The thing hissed as it looked with rage on the procession below.

People began to scream in fear, and the mounted guards drew their swords looking to their captain for orders as they tried to keep their horses calm. But Raneous, now glowing with the light of heaven, reared up and declared back, "NO MURMEL! You have tried to bring destruction to this city, but have failed! The High King reigns here, for He is strong in the praises of His people!"

Raneous turned to face the people and the king and queen, and they gasped in wonder because his great feathery wings were now visible for all to see. He shook his white mane and with a toss of his head said, "Your battle is not against your king or each other, good Livians! This demon, called Murmel, has poisoned your minds. Sing for your deliverance!"

Myran motioned for Tabitha, his wife, and he quickly pulled her up behind him on his mare. He began to sing in a rich strong voice with Tabitha joining in perfect harmony.

The voice of the King is powerful!
The hand of the King is mighty to deliver!
He makes our feet to skip over trouble and he puts our feet
On firm ground.
We call out to our King and he answers us!
He delivers us from darkness!
And his mercy endures forever!

Mick stepped forward and began to accompany them with his flute, and the music filled the air once again. Others began to join in until it seemed the whole city was singing.

"STOP!! STOP THAT NOISE!" The evil Murmel screamed from his perch and in his rage he leaped off the tower to attack Myran and Tabitha, but Raneous and Brian leaped into the air to meet him. Brian raised his sword and to his surprise it was twisting in flames.

"The sword of song and praise!" The High King whispered to his spirit.

The three clashed in mid-air over the center of the marketplace. The impact was so strong Brian nearly lost his hold on Raneous. Raneous was in full battle mode and struck savagely with his powerful front hooves at the raging Murmel as Brian, now reseated, slashed hard at the thing's snake-like neck as it tried to claw at Raneous' chest. Murmel was too quick, however, and turned at the last minute. The flaming sword severed its right wing instead. The black leathery thing fell in flames, landing in the marketplace fountain. The demon screamed as he spiraled to the ground on just one wing, but not before he managed to rake his sharp claws over Raneous' hind quarters.

The evil claws ripped deep into the muscle and Raneous screamed in pain as bright red blood stained his white coat, but he followed the demon to the ground, with people scattering in all directions. Even in all this chaos the singers kept on singing as the white winged horse and the demon of darkness battled.

Praise, Praise the High King!
His mercy endures forever and ever!

"COME TO ME! YOU OFFSPRING OF THE DARKLANDS!" Murmel screamed loudly as he spread his claws out and beckoned. Brian glanced quickly around and saw to his horror rats and snakes and smaller demons crawling slowly to him.

"What's wrong with them?" Brian asked more to himself than to anyone, but Raneous answered.

"They are weak! The songs of praise steal their strength and Murmel has been grounded!" Raneous kept his eyes on Murmel as they circled one another in the market square. Brian felt the horse's body tremble beneath him and noticed he was favoring his back leg. Anxiously he looked back at Raneous' wound. Bright blood dripped freely from five wicked slashes in his flesh and down his back leg leaving small pools of blood where he stood.

"Raneous! You're hurt!" Brian swallowed hard. Was this even possible? He thought Raneous was undefeatable. Fear began to clutch at his heart. *"What if…"*

"MURMEL! You have lost! You and your kind must leave this city!" Raneous declared firmly as he locked eyes with the red-eyed reptile.

"Not so fast! You think I'm defeated that easily?!" It hissed and it flicked its black forked tongue at the horse and boy. It's eyes burned red. " Ha! Look to the North and MELT with fear!"

Raneous and Brian looked up at the northern storm clouds that were boiling and rolling unnaturally. As they watched, Brian gasped in dismay. Hundreds – maybe thousands - of winged demons were emerging out of the clouds! It looked to be thousands of them! They could hear the beating of their leathery wings and see the wicked gleam in their eyes as they prepared to descend upon the city. Brian's heart sank. So many of them!

"High King! Save us now!" he prayed.

"MINE!!!" Murmel screamed and he lunged for the horse's throat.

"LOOK!!" was all Brain could say before it struck, but it was enough and Raneous turned his body causing the demon to miss and bite into his shoulder instead. Brian, however, was able to quickly beat Murmel back with his sword saving the horse from more serious damage.

The Captain of the Guard sprang into action. He was no fool, but he also knew that this was no ordinary fight. His sharp eyes had picked up the enemies' weakness. With his sword raised to the heavens he gave his orders, "Swords drawn! We march in formation around the perimeter of the square! We must sing with the singers!"

"Wait!" a small but firm hand grasped the captain's reins. He looked down in surprise into the steady blue eyes of Anna the Prophetess. She smiled and handed him what looked to him like an ancient but beautifully polished ram's horn. "Please! Use this. It's powerful in times of war. Each time you circle the square give a long blast and have your men shout!"

With a quick nod he urged his mount forward, raised the horn to his lips and blew a long blast! A loud and commanding trumpet call erupted from the simple instrument. His men behind him drew their swords and began to join in the song of praise as they marched on horseback around the square. With the completion of one circle the captain drew his sword and raised it high. "Now shout!" he commanded and he blew the horn again with a great long blast. The demons in the city recoiled with the shock of it and even Murmel trembled where he crouched. Twice and then a third time the king's guard circled in song and then shouted with the blast of the ram's horn.

"Look!" Brian cried. He and Raneous were still in a standoff with Murmel. The demon lord, however, was now waiting for reinforcements and not anxious to engage them. Raneous looked up to see thousands of demons drop from the black clouds, but instead of descending upon the city, they reached a certain point just above the highest castle tower and were stopped in mid-flight like they had hit an invisible shield or bubble over the city. "It's working! They can't attack!" Brian was elated.

At the sound of the guard's third great shout, a ray of sunshine broke through the heavy clouds in the eastern sky and Raneous, with his sharp Brightlander eyes, caught a beautiful sight! Suddenly, he found new strength and he faced the demon once again.

Now Murmel! Now YOU look to the East and know that your destruction is sure!" Raneous said with a toss of his great head and a stomp of his hoof.

The startled and enraged creature looked up in shock as thousands of winged horses armed with fighting angels broke through the clouds. They descended with great force upon the host of demons suspended helplessly over the city. Raneous saw a flash of white and with a surge of joy and wonder, recognized his own father, Palladon, charging forward with Michael the Archangel on his back. Together they plowed through hundreds of terrified, screeching demons. With one swing of the mighty angel's sword, darkness was giving way to light!

The angelic host filled the sky over Livia, the demon horde evaporating with a howl and a squeal with each swing of their blazing swords. The blaze of light, the thunder of beating feathered wings, was beyond words to describe, as it exploded the senses, but without a doubt the evil that had tried to strangle Livia was being cut down.

"NO!!!" Murmel writhed in fury and blindly lunged again at the white stallion in front of him. But Raneous and Brian were ready. Raneous caught the demon on the underside of its chin with his hoof causing its head to be thrown back.

"Now, Brian! Finish him!"

In that instance, the snake-like neck was fully exposed. Brian leaned forward and with a downward swipe with the flaming sword and renewed strength, he beheaded the awful beast. The head hit the cobblestones as the black ooze spurted from its mouth and severed neck. It flopped once or twice as it came to rest against the fountain.

The songs of praise erupted into shouts of joy and celebration, and behind the castle the ancient crypt's door burst open. From deep inside the stink hole, all the missing people from Livia came to themselves and began to slowly make their way into the castle yard blinking at the day and wondering what had just happened. The High King had won the city! Rhyse and Roslyn, along with many others, were jumping up and down and hugging each other in the middle of the square.

"We Won! We Won!" they shouted to each other over and over.

Raneous, standing over the beheaded demon, caught a shining glimmer in the clouds overhead and looked up. His heart leaped in joy as he saw his mother, Radiance, with none other than Kiran, the mighty warrior, on her back. Kiran raised his sword in salute to Raneous before they streaked off like a shaft of light. Joy pierced with loneliness shot through Raneous' soul. Once again, he was left behind in the mortal realm. A longing filled his heart as he looked yearningly at where his mother had been. She was gone and he was here victorious but wounded and bleeding; a lone Brightlander among mortals.

"Look! Look to the walls of the city!" Roslyn excitedly pointed to the outer walls of the city. Now another wonder could be seen by all. Large, twelve-foot angels, with faces like chiseled marble, and robes of radiant white, stood on top of the thick stone walls of the city completely encircling it. Each angel had a magnificant white eagle sitting on his right shoulder. All the angels except one, that is. This one angel's face was covered with the hood of his robe and in his right hand, he lifted a golden balance scale.

"The scales of judgment!" whispered Raneous in awe as he pushed his lonely thoughts aside.

The sky had cleared and the spectacular battle overhead was finished. The storm clouds had evaporated with the surge of the angelic host upon the dark forces. Now clean sunshine shown down on the city of Livia, but as the citizens saw the solemn angelic judge lift his scale, silence swept over the crowd. The Captain of the Guard and his men dismounted and removed their helmets in respect. The city waited. King Jerald, still on the balcony, shakily dropped to his knees, his yellow hands holding tightly to the railing. Queen Vanora, however, was nowhere to be seen.

A voice like thunder came from the hooded being. "The citizens of Livia have been found guilty of many serious crimes against each other and against their king. The poison from your tongues opened the doors to the Darklanders to deceive your minds and bring your city to the brink of destruction through division and chaos."

Many of the Livians now dropped to their knees and bowed their heads as they knew in their hearts they were guilty. Now that the city was saved, would it now be doomed by its own guilt?

The angel continued. "The praises of the High King's servants, their repentance for the state of their city, and their celebration of the High King in the face of darkness has delivered this city from the Great Dragon's clutches, for the High King is ever merciful." The scale in the angel's hand tipped to the right. "Therefore, this city has been granted complete deliverance for the sake of the High King's own. Release the eagles!"

The eagles were launched from the shoulders of the angels and they circled the city on their great wings. All the angels raised their hands over the city. As they did so, every rat, snake and any other dark creature was compelled out of its dark hiding place. Hundreds of them filled the streets hissing and spitting savagely. The mighty eagles descended on them with their powerful talons and beaks. The sight was gruesome as well as wonderful. In a few moments, not a snake or a rat from the Darklands remained in the city of Livia.

The angel of judgment lowered the scales. "Livians, honor first your High King, honor second your ruling king, and thirdly honor each other."

The citizens of Livia answered in unison. "All of this we will do!"

When the angel heard this response, he lifted his arms towards heaven and all the angels faded from view. All the Livians stood speechless in wonder and awe at what had just happened. But as the realization sank in that they were truly free, people began to smile and hug each other. The Captain of the King's Guard, mounted his horse and blew the ancient horn once again causing everyone to look to him. He then turned his mount to face the king's balcony.

"Long Live King Jerald!" he shouted.

The citizen's of Livia echoed their heartfelt response, "Long live King Jerald! Long live Queen Vanora!"

Then it became apparent. Where was Queen Vanora?

25- TREASON

What indeed had become of the queen? In order to answer this question, it's necessary to go back to what has happened with Sam. Sam, true to his word, had found a very nervous Roslyn waiting inside the tower as far away from the dead snake as she could be. He had quickly introduced himself and presented her with the pouch. With a quick curtsey, she had returned to the queen's chambers with Queen Vanora never the wiser.

After some thought, Sam decided to keep himself hidden from the queen. If she figured out that he had betrayed her, she would most likely make him disappear for good. Quickly, he made his way down to his old sleeping quarters and managed to avoid being recognized by anyone. Once in his room, he locked himself in and didn't even come out when the fire broke out in the stables. He knew a lot – too much- about the queen's plans to bring Livia under a new government, to dare show his face now. It was best to stay hidden. However, he didn't know everything. As he lay in his bed in the dark listening to all the noise and commotion going on around the castle, he thought about King Jerald. He had observed that the king's health was declining and he suspected something was not right, but until now he had been too focused on his own pursuit of power to care about the king. Sam now gave it his full attention and the more he thought the more he saw the obvious truth.

"I have been an idiot! Of course Vanora was going to take out the king! She would have to in order to change the order of government. I have been a blind fool!"

High King," he moaned in the dark as he lay in bed. "How can you forgive me for this? I can hardly forgive myself! We need proof of Vanora's betrayal to her husband. We need evidence. I myself should be hung for treason, but I would dearly love to make it right and see justice for King Jerald!"

Somewhat to his surprise, an image of an elegant wine decanter appeared in his mind. It looked familiar. He had seen it before. It was etched crystal with silver. Amethyst jewels in the form of grape clusters cascaded down its sides. Then it clicked and he remembered. The queen had given it to the king as a birthday present a year ago. The king enjoyed a sweet dessert wine after dinner and the queen would make a ceremony of bringing it to him herself and personally pouring it for him. It was all very sweet and the king loved the attention. Now the question was where was this wine decanter? It was the king's technically, but the queen always kept it with her. Then Sam sat right up in bed. There was one place no one was allowed except her. A room where no one had the key except the queen. Sam smiled in the dark. "No one else has a key – except me!"

*

Sam arose early the next morning. The king and queen would be dining in the banquet hall for a special birthday breakfast before the parade. This was his chance! Sam waited until he heard all the servants make their way to the banquet hall. Quickly and quietly he found his way up the back servant stairs to the hall of the queen's chambers. All was quiet. He walked briskly past the dressing rooms and came at last to a very plain door on the right. Glancing quickly around, he pulled out his key ring from under his cloak and selected a very plain looking key. He slipped it into the lock and turned. "Click!" The door opened quietly inward to reveal the queen's personal library. It was a small room lined with books on all of the walls. Sam looked around and noticed a small writing desk in the corner. As he made his way to it, he scanned the shelves filled with books and stopped at a large leather book that looked like it had been carelessly misplaced. *Potions and Poisonous Plants* it read.

"Hmmm. Interesting reading for a queen."

He reached the small desk. Writing instruments and parchment paper littered the top. He pulled open a deep bottom drawer and gasped. "There it is!" The king's wine decanter was sitting down in the drawer. Carefully, he pulled it out. It was about half full of a deep red wine. Slowly, he lifted the crystal stopper and took a tentative sniff. It smelled of sweet, fruity wine and…something else. His head began to ache a little. Carefully, Sam replaced the stopper and set the decanter on the desk. He began to look through the other drawers but found nothing. He looked again in the top drawer. This time he reached all the way to the back and to his surprise touched something soft and velvety. He grasped it and slowly pulled forth a black velvet drawstring pouch. Sam's heart beat quicker as he loosened the strings and peered in. A glass vial with a cork stopper nestled within. Gingerly he pulled it out, sat down and ever-so-carefully pulled the cork. The sweet spicy fragrance wafted into his nostrils. Such a wonderful smell! But Sam's head now began to throb and he quickly put the cork back on. Memories of King Jerald's first wife, Helen, came rushing into his head with the smell of this fragrance.

"Oh no!" Sam realized the truth. This was the same fragrance that the first queen had loved to wear – the same perfume that Vanora had given to her as a gift. Sam rubbed his forehead. He took another whiff of the wine. Yes, now it was unmistakable, the faint sweet spicy fragrance was in the wine as well. Out loud he said, "So it was not perfume allergies I had when I worked with Queen Helen. It was a reaction to poison!"

Quickly, he replaced the stopper on the wine decanter. He had everything he needed to prove Queen Vanora's murder of poor Queen Helen and her murderous intentions for King Jerald. He should have seen it long ago with as much inside information as he had, but he had been blinded by greed.

"Forgive me, High King for my selfish pride! I ask again for you to help me make at least some of it right!"

*

Meanwhile, while Sam was exploring, King Jerald and Queen Vanora had made their way from their breakfast to the balcony to see the parade and closing ceremonies. The king was visibly tired from all the activities. Queen Vanora, against her lady-in waiting's advice, had draped her pet python around her neck. As she and the king sat on well cushioned thrones on the balcony, she stroked its dry scaly body. "Soon, my lovely, very soon all will be accomplished!" she cruned to the reptile.

The crowds began to cheer as the mounted horses and the guard came into view. Slowly the king stood and with a sigh the queen did as well. She smiled and waved solemnly as the procession moved into the market square.

Her snake gave a twitch and it turned suddenly with a flick of its tongue. Its head began to weave back and forth, not in pleasure but in agitation, constantly flicking its tongue. Vanora looked with curiosity at the rest of the processional. What an amazing sight they were- dancing and singing with all their might! Soon she caught the words of the song and she realized that they were not celebrating the king's birthday; they were praising a High King! The King of Kings! At that moment, the python threw itself from her shoulders in a panic and slithered hastily back into the castle trying to get away from the dreaded and powerful vibrations of praise.

Queen Vanora moved to go after it, but she could not leave her post, so she stood and fumed at the dancers and singers who were causing such a disruption in things-her things!

Then the demon Murmel had appeared!

"My master!" She had breathed in excited surprise. "Today is the day... It's today!" For a moment she was afraid. Why didn't she know? Had she missed a message from Thorndike? King Jerald wasn't dead yet. She was going to finish him off tonight. In his weakened state it wouldn't take much. Quickly she recovered herself always confident in her abilities. Well, if she had missed something she would make up for it. It was fast becoming open war over the city. This was not supposed to be hard. Thorndike had taken over Norwin effortlessly.

"The snake! I must release the great snake from the crypt! Murmel will be pleased with that! And victory will then be ours!" Vanora turned, ignoring the king, and ran quickly through the castle hall. She was not alone, however. Rats! Hundreds of black rats were scurrying and hissing. A few snakes slithered past her as well. All were getting away from the music. Vanora rounded a corner and nearly ran into Sam.

Surprised at seeing him out of the crypt she said angrily, "Why aren't you in the crypt? We need to release the snake!"

Sam just looked at her trying to remain calm. Puzzled, Vanora realized he was no longer in his priest robes. Her eyes fell on the wine decanter in his hand. He had just come from her library!

"It's over Vanora. Your treason has been exposed."

Vanora stared at him in shock and anger and then screamed with her fists clenched and her face red, "My treason? You mean your treason! You have betrayed ME!" Vanora's beautiful face twisted in an ugly rage. "And it's not over!" she continued, her green eyes flashing. "The great Murmel is here to take the city and I must release the great snake!"

"It's dead." Sam said softly, still not moving.

Vanora's eyes grew wide with fear and anger. She inhaled sharply in disbelief. "No! Impossible! You lie!" She roughly pushed past him and ran to the back staircase where she stopped and declared savagely. "I will free it myself! And I will deal with you later!"

At that moment her pet python came slithering in a panic down the hall. It spotted her and quick as lightning wound itself up her body. The unexpected motion set her off balance and she stepped backwards, catching her silver heel on the hem of her rich gown. The snake, in its effort to cling to her, had covered her eyes with its scaly body. Teetering backwards blindly, Vanora waved her arms around madly, trying vainly to find something to grab. With a bloodcurdling scream, she toppled over and fell headlong down the steep spiral staircase.

Maria, the lady- in-waiting, who had followed the queen from a distance, heard her scream and came running. She and Sam reached the top of the stairwell at the same time. They both looked down in shock and horror at the queen as she lay crumpled in a heap at the first turn in the staircase. Maria clutched Sam's arm for support as she gazed down at her mistress. Vanora's neck was twisted unnaturally and was obviously broken. Her lifeless green eyes stared upwards at nothing. Her precious snake, however, had survived the fall and was uncoiling itself from her lifeless body. A shadow suddenly cast itself over the snake as a great white eagle appeared at the open castle window above the stairwell. Its bright golden eyes locked on the snake and with a great flap it swooped down and seized the writhing and hissing python with its sharp talons and carried it swiftly away back through the window.

Sam stood speechless while tears streamed down Maria's pretty face. She whispered, "I somehow knew it would come to this. You dabbled in things you knew nothing about, my queen!"

Sam swallowed hard. He knew that his fate would have been death too, if not for his brother's determination to not give up on him. Sam's mind went to the king, still unaware of his wife's tragic death. Would the news kill him? He was so weak now. How could they break it to him?

Maria turned to Sam and wiped her eyes. She was already ahead of him. "We cannot tell the king yet! He is exhausted from his party. It won't be hard to stall for a day in his present condition. We must discuss the situation with trusted advisors -those that were not working in her schemes."

Sam, with some surprise, realized that Maria was actually loyal to the king and not the woman she had spent years in friendship with! He also realized that she knew that he was a king's man himself (he was now anyway). Maria smiled sadly, seeming to read his thoughts.

"All will be told in due time, but now we must get the queen's body to her chambers."

26- MARIA'S STORY

Three days had passed since the defeat of Murmel, the demon lord. During this time the king had been given much information concerning the plot against Livia and its rescuers. Now, King Jerald sat on his throne in the great hall. Sam stood at his right and Maria stood at his left. Sam and Maria had been working tirelessly to restore the king's health. Sam, on a hunch, had found the antidote in the *Potions and Poisonous Plants* book in the late queen's library. Already the king's skin color was less yellow, his hands less shaky, and his mind clearer. The king's eyes, however, carried a deep sadness in them. He had taken the loss and treachery of his queen well outwardly, but only time would heal his heart.

King Jerald looked up at the bright sunshine pouring in through the eastern windows and then slowly around at his loyal friends and subjects. There were twelve in all. Anna the Prophetess, Myran and Tabitha with the twins all stood patiently to his right. Mick (free of his handlebar mustache at last), Brian, Jonathon and Raneous stood to his left. Also to his left were three of his council members – all the others had fled with the defeat of the demon Murmel. King Jerald smiled when the white stallion met his gaze.

"I was right about you!" he said playfully pointing a bony finger at Raneous. "You did indeed protect me!" Raneous' wings were again hidden, but everyone knew the truth about him now after his very public battle with the demon. Raneous bowed his head in acknowledgment to the king. The king's eyes clouded over in sadness and pain again. "May all my future decisions be just as wise." He turned to Sam. "The queen…She has been properly buried?"

Sam cleared his throat, "Yes, Your Majesty, she has been properly and respectfully buried in the crypt as you requested.

"Good!" the king paused. "But this is not a time for mourning! We will not mourn a traitor! We are here this morning to give honor where it's due and make decisions that will start a new, fresh beginning." Here the king turned to Maria, Vanora's former lady-in- waiting. "You promised to help us understand, Maria. Please tell us all what you know and who you are.

Maria stepped forward, to address the small group. "I am Maria of Norwin, daughter to Omar the Prophet." She smiled warmly at Jonathon, "Jonathon is my youngest brother. We both grew up in the king's court as my father, Omar, was the Norwin king's close councilor. There was another councilor that had much influence on our king and his name was and is Thorndike. Vanora was his niece and was mentored by him. She and I, both young girls in the king's court, became fast friends. Vanora was beautiful, intelligent and very skilled at influencing others. Over the years she began to spend more and more time with her uncle under his private tutoring. About three years ago, changes began to happen in the king's court and the king began to act strangely. My father sensed something was wrong, but the king began to shut him out of his council and listen solely to Thorndike. Norwin then began to have a rat infestation. About that time Thorndike had instructed Vanora to make contact with Queen Helen of Livia, send her gifts and become her friend, if possible. Now we know that one of those gifts, the perfume, led to her death and thus opened the door for Vanora to become queen."

The king placed his hands over his face, "My poor, poor Helen! But go on, I must know. Go on."

Maria continued, "As we all know, it worked. Being Vanora's best friend, I was chosen as her lady- in-waiting. Of course I was unaware of these hidden things. Vanora was working in secret with Thorndike. They were full of visions of power for themselves as they aligned themselves with a darker force at work disguised as the Unity Council. My first loyalty is and always will be to the High King and to his service. My father and I stayed in contact these last two years and we began to see parallel patterns happening in both kingdoms. The rats and snakes, the sickening of the ruling power, the chaos and division from within. Then last week, the Norwin king died and Thorndike has now declared himself Governor Thorndike. My father and I knew that Thorndike and Vanora were communicating regularly, so my father instructed Jonathon to keep watch for the messenger. So when Jonathon saw Thorndike's trusted assistant on horseback heading south, he overtook him and was able to seize the letter. Thorndike, in his foolish pride, had become careless and had sent a very dangerous message to Vanora. I have the message here."

Maria pulled a scroll from her waistband and unrolled it.

"My dear Queen Vanora and lovely niece,
The time has come! I have now begun the transfer of power in Norwin. The king is dead.
King Jerald must soon follow. Why wait? The timing is perfect! I understand the king
has a birthday coming up. Instead, it will be his funeral. The day after the funeral,
proclaim yourself ruler. You have everything you need, for I have taught you well.
In service to The Great One,
Thorndike"

Maria closed the scroll back up. "Of course, thanks to my brother, this message never made it to the queen. King Jerald would already be dead if it had. But the High King in his mercy has spared Livia and now we are hopeful that Norwin too can be taken back from the enemy. Now we know how to fight against this particular kind of evil. I suspect that with Murmel, the demon lord, destroyed, the power over Norwin is greatly reduced. We have learned much here thanks to you." Maria bowed to Raneous.

Everyone remained quiet for a moment digesting this new revelation. The king spoke first as he slowly stood to his feet. With a voice filled with emotion he prayed,

"High King over all, forgive me of my foolish blindness. Thank you for your mercy and give me the wisdom of your kingdom so I can rule Livia rightly." The king then addressed everyone. "I can in no way ever repay you for the grave danger that you put yourselves in on my account and for the sake of Livia, but I can give you honor." He clapped his hands and a paige boy carrying a silver chest came forward. The king opened the chest and drew out a golden medal hanging from a golden chain.

"Maria of Norwin, faithful servant and friend to justice! You have saved my life – you and your father. You are free to return to Norwin with your brother. My doors will always be open to you and should you wish to return to my courts here, you would be welcome." The king draped the medal over Maria's elegant head. Maria curtseyed but did not speak as her eyes were shining with tears.

The king turned to the former serpent priest. "Sam! You have been ransomed like I have been. I now give you full pardon for your betrayal to the throne in light of your complete change of heart and valiant service to me these last few days. I welcome you to my council free and clear of all crimes." Sam knelt and kissed the king's hand.

"Thank you, Sire. I don't deserve it, but I am grateful and pledge my life in service to you and to the High King."

The king then turned to the prophetess as he drew another gold medal from the silver chest. "Anna the Prophetess, you have been faithful through to the finish!" The king draped the medal over her strawberry blonde head. "I invite you to be on my council. I need those around me who hear the voice of the High King! With you and Sam by my side, I have hope for a brighter future."

The king slowly drew out four more golden medallions. "Myran and Tabitha! You risked your careers and positions for your city! We all have a new appreciation for the power of music and dance! Your children, Rhyse and Roslyn, have shown themselves brave and resourceful in the midst of danger. With your family in the lead, I hope that you will bring a new level of life to this city! Well done all of you!"

Brian wanted to applaud and whistle but it seemed that this was a solemn moment, so he kept quiet. The king slowly moved to his left and laid a hand on Mick's shoulder. "A loyal and brave Livian and one not easily defeated. Thank you for listening to the High King, for you not only saved your brother, but you saved all of Livia!" Tears welled up in Mick's eyes as he fingered the gold medal around his neck. King Jerald continued, "I still desire you to be my personal minister of music. Your pipes touch my heart like no one else I have heard. In light of your great service to Livia, I also give you the choice of remaining in my Mounted Guard or not. We can later discuss where best to use your gifts ."

"Thank you Sire, the honor is mine." Mick bowed to the king.

"Jonathon! Faithful northern neighbor! I can never repay you or your family for saving Livia even when your own city is even now in peril. Your father, Omar, has my pledge of support. I will send whatever resources to his aid that may be called for. We can discuss this in depth later." Jonathon bowed as the king slipped the golden chain over his dark hair.

Brian's heart beat faster as he realized his turn was up. The king looked at Brian and smiled, "So, the white horse comes with a stable boy, heh? More like a winged horse from heaven comes with a valiant young warrior!" Brian blushed crimson but managed to bow as the king hung the gold chain around his neck. The gold piece shimmered as he looked down at it. "May the strength of the High King always be in your arm. I also officially release you from any further service to me as I understand that you have come from the Borderlands to aid us. I am forever in your debt."

"You're welcome, Sire. It was my pleasure." Brian answered with some relief as he thought about his parents and the farm waiting for him.

"Ah! Now we get to our beautiful, noble white horse!" The king once again placed his hand on Raneous' forehead. "Raneous, I have never spoken to a horse that had the power of speech, but then I have never seen a flying horse from the heavens either. You were the secret weapon here. And as much as I would love to be selfish and keep you here, I understand that you are owned by no one but the High King himself, and so I also release you from any further service to me." The king paused and looked into the intelligent liquid eyes. "You were the beginning of my healing there in the stables. There is no way I can ever repay you, but Anna our Prophetess and new council member has something for you, I am told." The king turned beckoned to her with his jeweled hand.

Everyone watched curiously as Anna and three young court maids approached Raneous carrying beautiful orange satin ribbons. Raneous shifted his back leg as his wound, though cleaned carefully, still ached and throbbed from time to time. Anna smiled warmly at Raneous and said, "I can't claim to understand what exactly this means, but the High King instructed me last night in a dream that I was to decorate your mane and tail with orange ribbons. "He said," Anna closed her eyes as she tried to remember the exact words, "Orange, for you have brought the power of God through the joy of praise!" Even while she was speaking the three girls had been busily braiding and twisting the ribbons into his fabulous mane and tail.

Raneous bowed his regal head to King Jerald, "The High King guides us all - each in our own place. We each served a part and the salvation of this city could not have happened without any of you. The unity of everyone's gifts coming together broke the power of the enemy." Then Raneous said simply, "I'm glad I could be of help."

Everyone smiled at that humble remark from a heavenly Brightlander. The king then announced, "Now, it is my honor to present you to the people of Livia as heroes – for that is what you are. You are to be mounted on our finest horses – except you, Raneous – and you shall ride through the city of Livia with my Mounted King's Guard and all their fanfare. The people of Livia would love to have the opportunity to celebrate you!

Once this day of celebration is over, I believe Maria and Jonathon must ride north to their father. Myran and Mick have volunteered to go with them to help gather the High King's servants together to move against the evil infestation in Norwin. Maria has informed me that the Norwin king has an heir, though he is young. It is hoped that once Thorndike is taken out of power, that under the tutelage of Omar, this young heir will become a wise ruler." The king turned and looked at Raneous and Brian. "You of course may go with them, but I do not presume to give you orders on that matter."

Brian looked at Raneous and whispered, "Are we going to Norwin?"

"It is my understanding that I have done my part in this." Raneous whispered back. "We are going home, I think."

"Home!" Brian suddenly felt homesick for his family and the small farm they worked. Yes, it felt right. "Can we leave tomorrow?" he urged. Then he caught sight of Rhyse and Roslyn. He had made some good friends here in Livia. Brian suddenly felt torn. "Well, maybe not tomorrow." He would miss the twins and he didn't have many friends at home. Goodbyes are always hard. However, he hadn't left yet and today would be something to remember. Maybe he'd see them again. He looked over at Roslyn who caught his look and smiled. Brian smiled back. Yes, he really, really hoped to see her again!

27- HEALING OF THE HEART

The sun was peaking over the eastern hills behind the castle. The town of Livia was mostly still asleep after all the excitement of the last few days, but a sense of peace lay over the city like a warm blanket. Brian and Raneous were at the town livery watching Mick, Jonathon and Myran saddle their horses to leave for Norwin. Maria would be meeting them at the castle. Brian was feeling out of sorts with everyone going in different directions now, but he could not deny that he wanted to go home.

Mick looked over at him as he tightened the girth on the saddle of the beautiful dappled gelding the king had graciously given him. "Hey, don't look so down! You know, Livia is really not that far. You and your family need to come for the fall festival. You can all stay with me.

"Or me!" Anna said cheerfully as she walked through the livery door just in time to hear the offer. "We are fast friends now. Bonded together in the service of the High King! That's the beauty…"

"HE'S GONE!" Ben came rushing into the livery wringing his hands and tears streaking down his young face.

"Who's gone?" Mick asked as they all looked with concern at the stable boy.

"Rune! The big red horse! The horse I was supposed to take care of! I'm such a failure!" he wailed. "We have to go looking for him before wolves get him or something. I came in just now to feed him and his stall gate was busted open. He must have kicked it through."

Raneous snorted and stepped up to Ben and nuzzled the top of the boy's head. "Ben, I assure you that Rune can take care of himself. He's been doing it for a very long time, though I guess it could be argued that he is not doing a good job in some ways. I promise that he won't be in danger of getting eaten by wolves. He comes from the same place as I do, but he has a deep hurt against the High King that has caused his heart to go cold." Raneous paused thoughtfully and then added, " But I can tell you this, Ben. Your selfless act of love for him in that fire hit a soft spot, and I believe there is hope for the old war horse yet. Don't worry, you've done a world of good for him.

"Really?" Ben wiped his eyes and looked at Raneous with wonder. "Okay, but I WILL miss him!"

"You never know, Ben, he may come back, but he may not." Raneous sighed. "I can assure you that he knows you love him and that's important."

Myran looked at the sun. "Well, we must be off. We need to make good time today and Maria will be waiting." Myran smiled at Raneous and Brian. "Thank you again for your aid in saving Livia. Now hopefully, with the High King's help, we can save Norwin. I guess that's the way it works, huh?"

Jonathon and Myran mounted, but Mick turned and gave Raneous and then Brian one more big hug. He then gave a nod and a bow to Anna, and then not knowing what else to do, quickly mounted his horse and started off towards the castle with the others.

"Now!" Anna turned to Brian with a smile before anyone could feel glum. "You two are to come with me back to my cottage and I will get you all situated for your trip home. I wouldn't want our heroes to starve before they made it back to the Borderlands. Though I am sure Essie at the castle would fix you up just fine, I want to do it myself. I think you need a break from all the people staring at you. I'll see if the twins want to join us for the day and you two can leave in the morning after a day of rest. My goodness! You do deserve a rest, I think."

*

The sun was deliciously warm on their backs as Anna, the twins, Brian and Raneous walked the small dirt road leading to Anna's cottage. They were all walking together, feeling a quiet joy and a happiness that comes with being with trusted friends and doing something worthwhile. With a lot of urging from Rhyse, Brian was telling Roslyn and Anna about their battle with the snake in the crypt and of Sam's rescue. Raneous was sniffing the breeze and relishing the smell of the apples from Anna's orchard, but dreaming wistfully of Brightland apples. He would interrupt Brian now and again to add a detail that Brian either forgot or felt might be boasting if he retold it. Suddenly, Raneous caught sight of a shimmering light in the trees to his right.

"Raneous! Come!" The voice in his mind was a familiar, loving voice.

Raneous stopped short and then everyone else stopped and looked questioningly at him.

"I need to meet you at the cottage later." And he took off to the right across the small field at a trot towards the thick woods. Brian noted with concern that he was still favoring his back leg.

"I hope he doesn't get some kind of infection." he muttered.

Before anyone could object, Anna moved the teens forward with suggestions for lunch. She had seen the glimmering light herself and knew Raneous had business to attend to. She also made a mental note to mix up a strong healing ointment for Raneous' wound.

Raneous reached the trees – mostly large oaks. There was not a lot of undergrowth, so he walked easily through the trees listening to the twittering of birds. Raneous came to a large grey boulder with green moss growing all over it and passed around it. That is where he saw them!

"Mother!" Raneous gave a happy whinny. Radiance, a beautiful velvet grey mare with silvery wings came forward and lovingly touched noses with him and laid her head across his strong neck.

"Welcome, my son!" She softly nickered.

Kiran, the angel, was there as well, sitting on a medium sized grey boulder. He stood and smiled at Raneous. "Welcome friend! The High King has sent us to give you a gift."

"Raneous bowed his head. "You two are gift enough!" Seeing his mother was the best gift of all. Being a Brightlander living in the Shadowlands for the High King was an honor, but it was lonely at times and sometimes he longed to be with other heavenly horses.

"The High King knows your heart, Raneous." Kiran said with a wink. "And so, Radiance is here. I think she is as happy as you are about it."

"The High King knows how to give good gifts!" Radiance said with a soft toss of her elegant head. "I see you are still wearing your ribbons. You look magnificent! I am so proud of you! It's not easy to win ribbons, you know."

"Everyone has insisted I wear them as long as I am in Livia. I think I will have Brian take them out when we leave tomorrow."

Kiran smiled again. "You are very much like your father in looks and strength, but I see so much of your mother's tender heart in you as well. It's a good mix. It's a powerful mix. But I am getting off track; we are bringing you a gift special ordered by the High King."

Raneous pricked his ears in curiosity, wondering what the High King could possibly give him.

Kiran, still smiling, reached down behind the boulder he had been sitting on and pulled up a silver basket full of red and gold apples from the Brightlands!

"For you only, my white friend! No sharing!" Kiran said as he placed the basket at Raneous' feet.

Raneous could hardly contain his happiness. The High King had known his secret wishes! He knew his longings and had granted both to him this day! In pure joy Raneous let out another whinny and kicked his back hooves in the air. He began to jump and frolic in celebration of his gifts and of the love and care he felt flood his soul.

"He truly sees me!" Raneous ran in a small circle like a young colt and tagged his mother by grabbing her mane in his teeth playfully. "Catch me!"

Radiance gladly tried and succeeded a few times.

And so for a little while, the three, two winged horses and one warrior angel, played tag in and around the great oak trees. Mostly on the ground, but sometimes one would take to the air as a quick maneuver. Kiran loved to somersault over the backs of the horses as they tried to tag him. Raneous, however, not to be outdone, caught Kiran's foot in his teeth as the angel somersaulted over the horse's head. Finally, satisfied with their game, they returned to the rock and Raneous settled down to enjoy his apples. Every crunchy juicy bite was heaven itself. Slowly he chewed, relishing every bite to its fullness as apple juice dripped down his whiskery chin. The good thing about Brightland apples is that a horse can't eat too many of them. They do not upset their stomach, so Raneous ate the whole basketful one by one.

Radiance watched him eat with a mother's tenderness. "My son," she said presently. "You are indeed supposed to return with Brian to the Borderlands for a short season. Live and work with them until the High King calls on you again. The battle is never far away. It can be in your own backyard or in another city or town. It is time for us to leave you now for a time, but you have friends here too. Love them! Don't be sad, because we will meet again."

Radiance gave her son a final nuzzle and Kiran mounted the mare and easily sat bareback. He raised his hand, "Until we meet again my friend!"

Raneous expected them to fly out of the wood but instead they faded from view. He was alone in the woods again, but instead of feeling lonely and abandoned, he was full of peace. The love of the High King had enveloped him and had bathed his lonely soul. He felt filled up and full of joy. With a start, he realized that the pain of his wound was gone and that he had been walking and playing without any thought to it! Feeling content, Raneous looked around at the quiet grassy glen he was standing in.

"I need to get back to my friends! Maybe Brian and the twins will be up for some tag!" He paused for a moment looking again at the soft grass. He was alone and no one was watching. On an impulse, the great stallion lay down and kicked all four legs up in the air. "But not before I have a really good roll!"

The End of Book Two

Index of Characters and Places

Characters:

Anna the Prophetess: Anna has a strong ability to hear the voice of the High King and has a deep understanding of how the unseen world and the seen world work together. She is the youngest sister of Tabitha and is Auntie Anna to Rhyse and Roslyn.

Becca: The mother of Brian and wife of her new husband Will. She has lost two husbands. One to a farm accident and the second to alcohol abuse.

Benjamin: The young stable boy who works in the King's Stables.

Brian: Having lost his father in a farming accident when he was ten, Brian had suffered abuse from his alcoholic uncle. During this time, he had found and befriended Raneous, a lost colt of the Heavenly Brightlands. Now thirteen years old, Brian has a new life on the small farm with his mother and new step father, Will. He is Raneous' closest friend and companion and his partner in this new adventure.

Demon: A servant of the Evil One or the Great Dragon. The Bible says they are fallen angels and that they rebelled against God. In this series, they are seen as black and scaly reptile creatures with sharp talons.

Essie: The castle's head cook. A plump and pleasant woman who is also a servant of the High King and friend to Anna the Prophetess.

Jonathon: A mysterious messenger from the north and son of Omar the Prophet.

King Jerald: The king over the Eastern Region of the Shadowlands. Lives in the city of Livia. He has a good heart but lacks wisdom.

Kiran: (Keer-un) A warrior angel from the Heavenly Host.

Myran: (Mi-run) The Director of the School of Fine Arts in Livia and a skilled acrobat. A man of great influence in the city and father to Rhyse and Roslyn. He is not a native of Livia, but came from the Southern Islands and met and married Tabitha. Together, they run the Fine Arts school in Livia.

Murmel: A dark lord of the Darklands and servant of the Great Dragon, or Devil. His specialty is division of people through negativity, gossip and hate. He comes to suffocate and restrict the goodness out of a people.

Michael the Archangel: Michael is a real angel mentioned in the Bible. He leads God's armies against Satan's (the devil) armies. He is a warrior and a protector.

Mick: A native Livian and a great musician of the flute. He has a real gift in bringing true worship to the High King. His brother, Sam, has disappeared and he is on a quest in search of him.

Omar the Prophet: The prophet of the Northern Region of the Shadowlands. Used to be a close counselor of the King of Norwin. Like Anna, he has a strong ability to hear the voice of the High King.

Palladon: (Pal-u-don) The father of Raneous and the swiftest and most powerful of the heavenly horses. He is a solid white war horse and ridden by Michael the Archangel.

Queen Helen: The first wife of King Jerald. A beautiful and gentle person, but died mysteriously of an unknown sickness.

Queen Vanora: King Jerald's second wife. Young, beautiful and ambitious, the new queen has a great talent for influencing people with her ideas.

Radiance: The wise and gentle mother of Raneous. A beautiful and strong gray mare with silver wings, she is a strong warrior for the Heavenly Host of Heaven.

Raneous: (Ray-nee-us) A beautiful white winged stallion, the son of Radiance and Palladon. In him is the strength of his father and the wisdom of his mother.

Rhyse: (Reese) A twin to Roslyn, his sister, and son to Tabitha and Myran of Livia. Rhyse is confident, cheerful and a boy who loves action. He is a skilled acrobat and tightrope walker.

Roslyn: A twin to Rhyse, her brother, and daughter to Tabitha and Myran of Livia. Roslyn is a dancer with a quiet confidence that balances out her twin brother.

Rune: A mysterious disillusioned war horse who has chosen to no longer serve the High King. His story is told in Book One-*Winged Horse of Heaven: Fallen.*

Sam: Brother to Mick and has disappeared. He worked in the castle as a spokesman for the king. He is the reason for the quest.

Tabitha: Wife of Myran and Director of the School of Fine Arts with her husband. She is over the dance school. Mother to Rhyse and Roslyn.

Tess: A handmaiden for Queen Vanora.

The Heavenly War Host: The armies of heaven. They are the angels and winged war horses that fight for the protection of heaven and the High King's children in the Shadowlands.

The High King: The Creator of all worlds; the Captain of the Heavenly Host. It is the name in this series to represent Jesus who became human and died so that we could be reconnected to our Father God.

Valtar: The Captain Valtar of the Darkland demons who was completely destroyed in battle by Raneous and Brian in the depths of the Darklands.

Will: The step father of Brian. He is a skilled farmer and a good man and husband. He is the third husband to Becca.

Places:

Heaven: A real place in the spirit realm. There is no evil in heaven. There God, his children and angels live.

Livia: (Li-vee-u) The beautiful capital of the Eastern Region of the Shadowlands. It is a city of the arts. Music, dance, song, painting,etc-it is the artistic center of the Shadowlands.

Norwin: The capital city of the Northern Region of the Shadowlands.

The Brightlands: The land of the winged horses, angels and others. It is where all is pure and unspoiled by evil. It is the heavenly realm just outside of heaven.

The Borderlands: This land is part of the Shadowlands that is closest to the Darklands. It is the darkest place to be in the Shadowlands because the evil forces are strong there. Brian's family farm is there and they have taken a great light into that area because they serve the High King.

The City of Glory: The beautiful golden city where God and all his people live in heaven.

The Darklands: The land completely controlled by evil. It can be underground or on top, and it can be represented by massive dark clouds of complete darkness.

The Shadowlands: The land of mankind. It lies between the Brightlands and the Darklands. It has both good and evil in it and is where the war for the High King's children is being fought. It used to be unspoiled by evil but is now in constant war between evil and good.

Songs:

All songs in this book are greatly inspired by one of the greatest song writers of all time, King David, author of the Psalms.

ABOUT THE AUTHOR

Robin S. McDonald graduated from Bellarmine University, Kentucky with a degree in Secondary Education and English. She now lives with her husband, two daughters, a beloved Australian Shepherd and an adorable Tonkinese cat in the great state of Texas.

Robin has always enjoyed a good story-especially one that opens up the imagination to new ways of looking at life. Christian fantasy has been an important aspect of her growth as a person and as a Christian both as a child and as an adult. Ironically, fantasy has been the avenue that God used to demonstrate to her His amazing reality. Through fantasy, God revealed to her His creativity in this world.

"Winged Horse of Heaven: Quest" is the second book of the series "The Raneous Chronicles". For those who fell in love with Raneous and Brian in the first book and for those who war for our cities and our countries on behalf of the High King.

THE RANEOUS CHRONICLES:

Book One: *Winged Horse of Heaven: Fallen*

Book Two: *Winged Horse of Heaven: Quest*

Book Three: COMING SOON!

If you enjoyed this book, please leave a review at Amazon.com.

For advanced notice of the publishing dates for Book Three, please provide your email at Raneouschronicles@gmail.com or contact the author on Facebook at Robin S McDonald-author. These books are also available as ebooks.